# MURDER IN WRITING
# ANNA CLARKE

CHARTER BOOKS, NEW YORK

This Charter book contains the complete text of the original
hardcover edition. It has been completely reset in a typeface
designed for easy reading, and was printed from new film.

MURDER IN WRITING

A Charter Book/published by arrangement with
Doubleday, a division of Bantam
Doubleday Dell Publishing Group, Inc.

PRINTING HISTORY
Doubleday edition published 1988
Charter edition/March 1990

ISBN: 1-55773-326-0

Charter Books are published by The Berkley Publishing Group,
200 Madison Avenue, New York, New York 10016.
The name "CHARTER" and the "C" logo
are trademarks belonging to Charter Communications, Inc.

PRINTED IN THE UNITED STATES OF AMERICA

10 9 8 7 6 5 4 3 2 1

# WRONG TURN?

They turned into a narrow road, and on a signpost she read, "Winsford—6." Not much longer now, but time enough for her to hear the end of the story of Gerald Alexander, which both ladies now appeared determined to tell her.

"The boat sank," said Jill. "He was sleeping, no doubt, and didn't notice the leak until it was too late. It was a bright but chilly autumn afternoon—rather like today—two years ago. Nobody else on the water. Nobody saw anything, so what really happened will never be known."

"Never be known," echoed Gloria. Her voice sounded rather slurred; was she having another attack?

That was Paula's last rational thought before the crash.

# 1

The sun was going down in a great glory of crimson and gold. On the main road running north of the cathedral city of Salisbury, drivers adjusted their mirrors and their screens, irritated by the splendour, unwillingly admiring.

The driver of a yellow mini, a slight fair woman of about forty, turned out of the line of traffic into a side road and positioned the car on the grass verge so that she could look at leisure. It was a picture-postcard view—Stonehenge in the sunset. On the previous occasions when Paula Glenning had come to visit her friend Frances Coles, she had been disappointed by the famous ancient monument. The stones had seemed to her dull and tamed, like zoo animals behind their wire fence, surrounded by sightseers with their cameras and their cars.

But now, from this vantage point, the stones showed up strong and clear against the fiery sky: the uprights, the crossbar, dark and mysterious, as they had stood for thousands of years. Scholars would argue forever about their origin and their meaning, but Paula, who taught English Literature to university students in London, felt no need to adopt any particular theory. It was enough to look and to wonder and to let the imagination roam.

Half past six. Frances was expecting her to dinner, and there was still some way to go along narrow winding lanes before she reached the village of Winsford, down in the valley.

It was quite dark when she got there, and she was grateful for the lights in the car-park of the Shepherd's Rest, which lit up the corner beyond which stood Frances's cottage.

Small, human-scale lights, thought Paula as she carefully backed the mini into the narrow driveway, but very comforting in the seemingly endless blackness of the October night. She was very much a creature of the city; she was glad her friend lived in the centre of the village, near the shops and the church and the well-patronised inn. When they built Stonehenge, she wondered, did they huddle together for safety and warmth, those primitive human creatures in that dark and boundless world?

She got out of the car and hurried along the garden path, suddenly craving for human company. It was odd that Frances had not come out to meet her. The light in the porch was on, and there was a rosy glow behind the sitting-room curtains. Perhaps she was upstairs, in the back attic bedroom where Paula would sleep; or in the bathroom, where she would not hear the car arriving.

Under the little trelliswork porch, still plentifully entwined with leaves of honeysuckle, Paula waited for an answer to her ring.

None came, nor was there any response to her second ring or to her knocking.

Had she perhaps mistaken the day?

No, of course not. They had spoken on the phone only this morning. Paula had said she did not need to go in to college tomorrow, Friday, and Frances had said, "Then come down tonight. I've got a creative-writing class going in a nearby village. We meet Friday mornings. In Lady Hindon's house. It's terribly feudal, but quite amusing. Would you like to come along?"

"Very much," said Paula, "if I won't be intruding."

"They'll love meeting you. They are very much impressed by academic learning."

"Are they very snobby? Do I have to dress up? Or wear a hat?"

"Heavens, no. Baggy tweeds. Gardening slacks. As long

as you don't actually tread mud into the priceless Persian carpets, anything goes."

"She's rich, then?"

"Very, but only fake-aristocratic. Her husband was some sort of business tycoon who gave a lot of money to Party funds. Keep off politics and you'll get on all right with her, Paula. She writes well and she's trying hard to improve. They've written short stories for this week's class. Some of them are very good."

The whole of the morning's telephone conversation flashed through Paula's mind as she stepped back onto the garden path and wondered what to do next.

She could either go over to the Shepherd's Rest and see if Frances was there buying a bottle of something to go with their dinner; or call the neighbours, with whom Frances might perhaps have left a message; or just sit in the car and wait till she turned up.

This last was the least appealing. If she was going to have to wait, she would much rather do it indoors. The lights of the inn were very inviting, but before taking refuge there Paula decided to go round to the back of the cottage. It was hardly likely that Frances would be gardening in the dark, but she might just have left the back door unbolted. Winsford was a law-abiding spot and people living in modest dwellings in rural areas did sometimes stick to the old country habit of not locking the door.

Paula left her suitcase in the porch, collected a flashlight from her car, and moved carefully round the side of the house. Behind the cottage the ground fell away steeply down towards the little river. Frances's garden consisted of a narrow grassy terrace just outside the back door, and then a sloping rockery, interspersed with two very steep flights of stone steps which led to a lawn and a vegetable garden on the level ground at the bottom. Paula had once nearly fallen on those steps, and was now very cautious of them, even in daylight.

It was very dark. There were stars in the sky, but no moon. The flashlight revealed only a small circle of ground. As Paula came round onto the grass outside the back door she became aware of something soft writhing round her ankle and at the same time she heard the cry for help. There was a moment of shock before she identified the softness as Frances's cat and the voice as that of Frances herself, not far away.

"Where are you?" called Paula, flashing the light onto the top of the rock garden.

"Bottom of the steps," came the reply. "It's my leg. It's not broken, but I'm finding it difficult to get up."

"I'm coming down," said Paula.

"Take care!" The strained voice was very anxious. "I tripped over something. I don't know what. Use the other steps."

"All right."

Paula walked along to the far side of the rockery, noting as she went that the back door of the cottage was ajar, and that from within there came the appetising smell of a chicken casserole.

"Take care!" cried Frances again.

"Okay. I'll hang onto the fence."

This was not easy. It was formed of wooden palings, placed close together. After nearly falling herself, Paula decided to abandon the flashlight and to hold on to the top of the fence with both hands, proceeding crabwise down the stone steps, worried about Frances but at the same time blaming her for the inadequacies of her back garden. Although Paula had to admit, in fairness, that on previous visits she had noticed that Frances always kept the steps clear of hazards and seemed to have no trouble with them.

Safe on level ground, she once again produced the light from her jacket pocket, and found her friend attempting to stand up.

"I'm covered in bruises," she said, "but I don't think there's anything more drastic than a sprained ankle."

Paula supported her on one foot. "Shall I go and get help? How about next door?"

"Bob and Susan are away in Spain, and I'd rather not ask anybody else. I think I can sort of crawl, if you'll come behind me with the light. I'm terribly sorry, Paula. What a welcome for you!"

Their progress was painfully slow. Frances pulled herself along by clinging to the stones in the rockery. Paula followed suit, reminding herself yet again that Frances knew her own treasured garden very well, every stick and stone of it.

And yet she had tripped and fallen. Why?

She asked the question aloud when they had reached the haven of the kitchen; Frances, refusing medical help, was bathing her ankle in a bowl on the floor while Paula made tea.

"I slipped on something," was the reply. "I don't know what. There's been no rain for days and the steps are quite dry."

"Snails? Slugs?"

"Oh no. I know those hazards."

"The cat?"

"Leslie?" Francis paused to stroke the big marmalade cat rubbing against her un-injured leg. "No. It wasn't him. I'll go and have a look in the morning and see if I can find anything."

"If you don't mind," said Paula, after they had drunk their tea and she had helped Frances to bind up her ankle and attend to the worst of the bruises, "I think I'll go and have a look now, before we eat. I do hate unexplained accidents, and if it rains in the night we may never know what tripped you."

Frances did not seem to be very keen on this suggestion. "If you are looking for a mystery, Paula," she said, "I promise you that Brookside Cottage, Winsford, is the last place you'll find one. My life here is an open book, as they say. Uneventful. Even monotonous. Though it suits me well enough."

Paula glanced with affection at her friend, who was now leaning back in one of the Windsor chairs with her leg propped up on a stool and looking tired, but in less distress than previously. She was about fifteen years older than Paula, and had been the teacher to whom Paula owed her own love of literature.

She was a vigorous-looking woman, big-boned, with strongly marked features and an air of competence. She was widowed and had one son, Andrew, who lived in London and about whom she always seemed to be anxious.

Paula never quite understood the reason for this anxiety, nor for the marriage having been so unsatisfactory. Frances had devised, perhaps only half-consciously, a very effective way of avoiding personal enquiries. Her references to her son and her late husband were made in a way that appeared to need no amplification, as if she simply assumed that Paula already knew all there was to be known about them, and Paula, taking her cue from her former teacher, was equally noncommunicative about her own affairs.

Their friendship was all the stronger for this absence of emotional exposure. They had great pleasure in sharing all the little things of life during the times they were together.

"I'm not suggesting that you have an enemy in the village," said Paula. "Not even some aspiring writer whose work you have slighted. I just want to know why you tripped. Maybe it's some fallen leaves."

"Maybe it is. Take the flashlight on the table in the hall— it's stronger than yours—and go down the steps by the fence, which seem to be all right. Then you can work up the others from the bottom. It's safer to come up than down."

"Yes, teacher," said Paula meekly. "And I promise to be very careful."

The descent was not too difficult, now that she was beginning to get the feel of the slope. If you lived here for years and went up and down these steps several times a day, you would indeed come to feel perfectly confident, even in the dark.

Paula turned the light towards the vegetable patch and the apple trees at the far end of the garden. Beyond them was a wire fence, and beyond that the grassy footpath that ran along the bank of the little river. By daytime it was a pleasant spot for people to walk their dogs and for children to play at the water's edge. At night it looked different. Mysterious, perhaps even menacing. Suppose there were somebody lurking in the bushes and watching her?

This uncomfortable thought made Paula hurry on with her errand.

The steps on which Frances had fallen were about two feet away from the left-hand border of the garden, which consisted of a wire fence intertwined with climbing plants. There was no firm hold to cling to, but the path itself was less steep than the one on the other side of the rockery. Presumably this was why Frances had chosen it.

Paula shone her light upon the lowest of the grey stone slabs. Here, and on the higher steps, were a few fallen leaves, brown and small and crinkled, that looked as if they had blown off the honeysuckle and clematis supported by the wire fence. It could not have been these that had caused Frances to slip. Neither could the tiny pieces of stone or grit that had seeped out from the rock gardens onto the sides of the steps.

By the time she was halfway up, Paula was beginning to

despair of finding any clues. Perhaps there had been a tennis-ball or a golf-ball lying there, and Frances's movements would have sent it flying away into the bushes. If so, it would have to remain there, because that was a search she was certainly not going to undertake in the dark.

Besides, she was getting very hungry, and Frances must be getting very impatient. They would simply have to accept that there was no particular reason for the accident, that Frances had just taken an awkward step.

Paula was still searching, but had given up expecting or even wanting to find anything, when she saw the dark patches on the steps near the top of the slope.

Mud? But everywhere else was perfectly dry. She placed the flashlight against one of the stones in the rockery, held on to one of the others for her own security, and with her free hand touched the dark patches. They felt cold and damp. Had somebody deliberately placed pats of slippery mud on these upper steps?

No. It was not mud. It was moss. Paula found a chunk of it, enough to be completely sure. She picked it up, retrieved the light, and hurried on into the kitchen with her find.

## — 2 —

The dinner had been eaten and Frances had hobbled into the living-room at the front of the cottage. This was warm and welcoming, with a coal-effect gas fire, red-shaded standard lamps, and old but comfortable chairs. Leslie, the marmalade cat, handsome against the dark green hearthrug, completed the picture of peaceful domesticity.

It was difficult to believe that somebody had wished ill to the owner of Brookside Cottage. Yet how else to account for that moss? They had talked of it during dinner and had returned to it again as they drank their coffee.

"I suppose it could have been dropped there by a bird," said Frances doubtfully. "Starlings or sparrows poking about on the roof. I've found bits of mud outside the back door. And dead leaves. The sort of stuff that collects in the guttering."

"But this isn't roof or drain dirt," protested Paula, "and it wasn't near the house. It was several yards away, and it's thick green moss. The sort of stuff you find in damp woods round the roots of trees. Look at it."

The specimen lay on a piece of newspaper on the low table next to the coffee tray.

"I've looked," said Frances, "and I quite agree that that is what I must have slipped on, but I can't agree that it was necessarily put there by human hand. There must be other explanations. Let's try to think of some."

8

It was as if they were back in the classroom, many years ago, with Paula, the keen pupil, being urged by her teacher to use her powers of reason.

"Is there any moss on the rockery?" asked Paula.

"No, not really," replied Frances after a moment's thought. "It doesn't stay damp enough. Too much wind and sun, and the water drains away down the slope."

"Have you got any moss like this in the garden at all?"

"Down at the far end. Under the apple trees. It gets very damp there." Frances shifted her injured ankle to a more comfortable position on the footstool. "If it weren't such an effort to walk, I'd go down and have a look now."

"You'd be able to tell if the moss had been disturbed?"

"Possibly. But not what had disturbed it. There's all sorts of wildlife around here. Foxes. Badgers. Rabbits. Hedgehogs."

"Would a fox or a rabbit or a badger or a hedgehog have dug up a great chunk of moss and put it near the top of the stone steps for somebody to slip on and fall when they came down in the dark?"

Frances had to admit that she thought this extremely unlikely. "Though birds nesting do drop the most surprising things about," she added.

"I don't know much about country life," retorted Paula, "but I've never heard of birds nesting in October. Do you think I might be able to learn anything from the roots of the apple tree if I go and have a look down there now?"

"I wish you wouldn't." Frances, usually so calm and confident, looked really anxious. "Truly I think it would be better left till morning. You would never be able to tell if the moss had been disturbed because you don't know how it looked before. And if there really is somebody lurking down there, then I wouldn't be able to get down to you if you needed help. Neither would anybody else, with Bob and Susan away on the one side, and Mrs. Barton barricading herself in from eight o'clock onwards on the other. Please don't do it, Paula. It worries me."

This was the first time, in all their thrashing around the subject, that Frances had openly admitted her anxiety.

Paula did not take much persuading. Her curiosity had led her into unpleasant, and even dangerous situations on several occasions, but there had always been some hope of a useful result. On this occasion she felt that she had already made the important discovery, and that any further foray into the garden tonight could only add to her friend's distress with nothing to show for it.

"I'm going to wash up," she said, picking up the tray. "Do you want to watch the news?"

"No thanks," was the reply. "But could you hand me that blue folder that's on the sideboard?"

Paula did so.

"Lady Hindon's writing class," explained Frances. "Some of them have brought me the short stories they wrote last week. I'd like you to see them, if you aren't too tired."

"Of course not. I won't be long."

But when Paula returned from the kitchen she could not help reverting to the subject still uppermost in her mind.

"Frances, were you really only going down the garden to fetch some parsley? I know there's no reason why you shouldn't. It's your garden and you lead your own life in your own way, and it's lovely to have herbs fresh-picked, but I can't help wondering—"

"Paula, you are right to wonder. I've been feeling guilty ever since you came, at not being quite frank with you. The truth is that I didn't want my accident to be anything but an accident. If there were anything suspicious, then I just didn't want to know, and I didn't want you trying out your sleuthing activities on it. But when you came in with that moss . . . I was shocked, Paula. The more I think about it the more uneasy I become. Yes, I did indeed go out to fetch parsley. I often go down to pick herbs or vegetables after dark. You get a different feel of the garden then, and the scents of things are stronger, and the steps don't worry me—I'm so used to them."

She paused for a moment, and shifted her ankle yet again.

"But tonight there was another reason," she went on. "I thought I heard something. When I was getting the dinner ready I looked out of the window and I had the distinct impression that there was somebody in the garden. I couldn't see anything. The kitchen light doesn't shine far enough, but I had the feel of it. That's why I went out. I'm sorry I didn't tell you before, Paula. Please forgive me."

"Nothing to forgive. At any rate it has made us go very thoroughly over all the other possibilities that might account for your fall. And reject them."

"And reject them."

They sat silent for a little while.

"Do you often have intruders in the garden?" asked Paula.

"Truthfully, no. I've been here twelve years now, and the only time I know of when somebody got over the fence was shortly after I'd moved in. I was teaching in Salisbury then and had got back from school early one afternoon. There were two ten-year-old girls systematically stripping one of the apple trees. My favourite Coxes." Frances smiled. "Little devils. They never did it again, nor did any other of the children in the village."

Paula smiled too. She could well imagine the scene. Mrs. Coles had always possessed a quality invaluable in a school-teacher, the ability to inspire both affection and respect.

"They are both at university now," added Frances. "They both send me Christmas cards."

"But whoever got in tonight—" began Paula.

She was interrupted by a ring at the front door.

"Rather late for callers," she said. "Shall I answer it?"

"Just a minute." Frances got up, clung to the back of her chair and pulled the window curtain a little aside. "It's only Bruce Wiley," she said, returning to her seat. "Lady Hindon's general factotum. He'll have been given some sort of royal command. Don't ask him in or tell him about my fall. Just say I'm busy, and take the message."

"Okay." Paula switched on the light in the porch and opened the front door.

The man who stood there was of medium height and could have been any age between forty and sixty. He was wearing a dark blue raincoat, and had very dark hair, on which raindrops were glistening in the light of the porch.

"Mrs. Coles not in?"

He had a pleasant voice and a friendly smile, and he had stepped over the threshold into the hall before Paula was aware that he was doing so.

Rather awkwardly, as if trying to halt a persistent sales-man, she moved between him and the door of the living-room.

"She's very busy at the moment," she said, "getting ready

for the writing class. I'm Paula Glenning. I'm staying with her over the weekend and hope to join her at Lady Hindon's tomorrow."

"Bruce Wiley." He held out a hand.

"You've got a message for Mrs. Coles?"

Paula knew that her question sounded stilted, and indeed she felt ill at ease. She believed herself to be totally free of any class prejudice, but nevertheless there was deeply ingrained in her, as in almost all English people, some need to know the social status of the person she was talking to, and she could not place Bruce Wiley at all. The voice and manner were those of a self-confident professional person, but she had a sense of falseness, as if he were acting the part, sending somebody up, perhaps.

"I've more than a message." From a pocket of the raincoat he produced a fat envelope. "I've got her homework for tomorrow's class. Lady Hindon's apologies for being so late with it, but she would be awfully grateful if Mrs. Coles could kindly glance over her composition."

Paula took the envelope. "I'll give it to her. I'm sure she'll be very pleased."

Had it really been a salesman, she would at this moment have tried to shut the door.

Bruce Wiley did not move. "So we'll see you tomorrow as well. That will be nice. But you mustn't expect high academic standards among the aspiring authors of Winsford and district."

"Do you come to the class yourself?" Paula felt obliged to make some comment, and this was the only remark that occurred to her.

"Sure. It's part of my job."

"We'll meet again, then."

He ought to have said "Goodnight" and departed; Paula, after a moment's hesitation, was just about to say "Goodnight" herself, when he spoke again, apparently with genuine concern.

"Is Mrs. Coles all right?"

"Perfectly," lied Paula, "but she's got behindhand because of chatting to me, and if she's going to read Lady Hindon's story too, we'd better leave her to get on with it."

"Sorry." Again came the friendly, lopsided smile. "I can

take a hint when it's as wide as a doorstep. I have to report to her ladyship, you see. She lives in a wheelchair, and I am her eyes and ears and all-round liaison person. In true feudal style, she likes to know what is happening in the village. Regards to Mrs. Coles. Don't come out. It's pelting down. Goodnight."

Paula watched the car move away before she shut and bolted the front door. Then she switched off the porch light, and returned to Frances.

"Did you hear all that?" she asked, handing over the fat envelope.

"Yes. I thought you did very well. There aren't many people who can get rid of Bruce Wiley so quickly."

"I wish you'd warned me."

"There wasn't time, my dear, and in any case one always finds out for oneself."

"The first rule of good teaching. But Frances, seriously, what are we going to do? I can quite understand that you don't want the news of your fall to go whizzing round the whole neighbourhood tonight, but they'll have to know about it tomorrow. That ankle is going to take some time to mend. I don't see how we can keep it quiet."

"I've been thinking about it all evening," said Frances, "and I've got an idea. But it depends on you being able to stay over till Monday. Maybe even till Tuesday. Is there the slightest hope of that? I hesitate to ask you. I know it's your busy time."

"I ought not to," said Paula slowly. "I suppose I could get somebody to take my classes for me, but there are a couple of meetings . . . oh, damn it, they'll have to go on without me. Why not? Other people take time off. If I were ill I wouldn't be able to get back. I'll have to say I've got 'flu."

"No," said Frances, "I'm the one who is going to have 'flu. Very badly. You will be looking after me. Won't that do?"

"It'll have to do," said Paula, beginning to understand. "You'd like to lie low here until you've recovered from your fall and then pretend it's never happened. I will do my best with your writing class at Lady Hindon's and with your other classes, and will ward off all enquiries. Is that the idea?"

"Yes," said Frances in a very low voice. "I know it's an awful lot to ask of you."

"But it isn't!" cried Paula warmly, putting an arm round her old friend, who suddenly seemed to her no longer the strong and self-confident teacher, but a worried and lonely and rather frightened woman. "It isn't a lot at all. If it hadn't been for you I'd never have gone to university and got a good degree and got a good job and—"

"You might have made a good marriage."

"Oh, let's not talk about failed marriages. I've almost forgotten mine now, and I've got a wonderful relationship with James Goff. Grandson of the novelist, you know. He teaches in my department. We get on fine." Paula hurried on, not wanting to talk any more about James, nor to hear anything of Frances's past. Their relationship was bound to embark on emotional confessions. "So that's settled," she said. "Give me a piece of paper and I'll make notes of what you want me to do."

Fifteen minutes later Paula said, "That seems straightforward enough. It's just the class tomorrow morning, and then Monday evening over at West Silworth. Do you think you'll be fit for your Women's Institute talk on Wednesday afternoon?"

"I'll have had five days to recover. Any remaining weakness can be attributed to the aftermath of 'flu."

"Okay. We'll see how it goes." Paula took the folder containing the students' stories. "I'll read these when I go up to bed. That settles your teaching obligations. Now what about social life? What would you do if you really were ill and I weren't here?"

"I would phone Bob Speedwell next door. He or Susan would do my shopping and fetch prescriptions from the chemist. They're a nice young couple. Unobtrusive but helpful."

"But they are on holiday in Spain. Who else would you ask?"

"Mrs. Barton, I suppose," said Frances reluctantly. "We've been neighbours ever since I came here, and are on good terms."

"But you don't want to get too deeply involved? She is a lonely elderly widow, and she would like to take over your life?"

"Well, not quite that. And she's really very kind. It's just that we haven't much in common. We have a cup of coffee and chat two or three times a week and the conversation always slips into the same two grooves. The husband who was such a wonderful mimic that he kept them all in fits of laughter, and the price of household goods."

"Does she have friends in the village?"

"Lots of acquaintances," replied Frances. "She goes to church and to all the women's meetings except in the evenings."

"Then I'll go and introduce myself to her tomorrow morning, and tell her you are ill and I'm staying to look after you, and she'll spread the news. Is there anybody else you'd like me to get in touch with?"

"No, I think that covers it."

How strange and how sad, said Paula to herself, that after all these years of living in Winsford, Frances should have no close personal friend here, no one but the neighbours and the people she meets through her work. Could it be that people were a little in awe of her, as Paula had once been? Or was it because she was reserved and deliberately kept them at a distance?

"I think we ought to call it a day," said Paula aloud, breaking into her own chain of thought, because after all, the question at the moment was not so much whether Frances had a close friend, but whether she had an enemy. "You need some rest," she went on, "and I've got all those stories to read."

Frances agreed, and Paula helped her upstairs. On the way, she said, "There's just two things that are rather worrying me. One is Bruce Wiley. How on earth do I get him to believe that you've got 'flu when I've just told him that you're very well?"

"He won't believe it," said Frances, pausing to rest on the landing. "There's nothing you can do about that. You tell your story and stick to it. I'm sure you'll be able to cope with Bruce. What is the other thing?"

"Your accident, of course, but we're not going to talk about that any more tonight."

Frances made no comment, but continued with her slow progress to her bedroom. "Goodnight, Paula. I can't tell you how grateful I am."

"Can you manage now?"

"Yes, thank you."

"Then call me if you need anything. I'll leave my door open."

At the door of Frances's bedroom, Paula stopped for a moment. "Oh, by the way, those students' stories. Did you suggest a topic for them? Did they have any particular assignment?"

"Yes. We've been discussing how to create suspense in crime and mystery fiction. They were to write a short story dealing with murder in a domestic setting."

"I see," said Paula thoughtfully. "Goodnight then. Sleep well."

## 3

It was well past midnight before Paula had finished reading all the students' work. Every story had some quality, and some of them were very good indeed—much better, thought Paula, than anything she could possibly write herself in such a vein. This was a sobering thought for someone whose job was to teach English Literature to university students, and Paula found that her respect for Frances, and her curiosity about the members of the creative writing class, were both considerably increased.

There were eight stories submitted, including the belated contribution from Lady Hindon. The remaining two members of the class had not been present when the assignment was given, but had promised to bring something along to read aloud at the next meeting.

Paula noted her comments against the list of names that Frances had given her. She thought for a moment or two about what she was going to say to the class and made a few notes for herself, and then replaced all the papers in the folder and got up and tiptoed into Frances's room.

There was no sound except that of quiet even breathing. Frances was fast asleep. Paula crept downstairs, not switching on the light, but using her little torch, partially shaded by her fingers, to guide her. In the kitchen she switched off the torchlight and stood for some while by the window, looking

out into the garden. The rain was falling steadily and there
were no stars to be seen, nor any lights from human habita-
tions. She could just make out the line of the fence to the
right, and the roses and honeysuckles that bordered Mrs. Barton's garden on the left. In the darkness straight ahead were
the apple trees and the bushes at the bottom of the slope.

As she looked, she could see an occasional slight lessening
of the blackness, where the rain was falling on the steps and
on the stones of the rockery. If I had not gone over it all
straight away, thought Paula, I would never have found that
moss. It would have been washed down the slope, or into the
earth round the plants in the rock garden, and we would have
had to assume that Frances fell because she missed a step.

Perhaps it would have been better that way, better not to
know that someone wished you ill, someone very near, who
knew your habits well; somebody with whom you believed
yourself to be on amicable terms.

If Frances had had the choice, she would have chosen not
to know, and Paula had done her no kindness by insisting on
investigating. But there was no going back now. Ignorance
once lost was gone forever, and in any case Frances had had
her suspicions even before Paula had found the moss. Not to
mention the fact that if somebody wanted her to have an accident, they would certainly try again.

Thus Paula reasoned with herself, but she could nevertheless not get rid of the feeling that she was bringing trouble to
her friend, and mixed with this irrational sense of guilt was
annoyance with Frances for being so secretive. Why had she
not said straight away that she thought she saw an intruder in
the garden? They could have called the police, and a doctor
for Frances, and everything would have been out in the open,
where Paula herself loved it to be. Surely that would have
been better than building up this complicated structure of deception that she had pledged herself to maintain?

The prospect was daunting, and reading the students' work
had not made it appear less so. There were some formidable
imaginations at work in the writing class. Could it possibly be
coincidence that two of them had chosen a fall down some
steps for their tale of domestic murder? One of these two was
Lady Hindon herself. The other was a retired parson, Rupert
Fisher.

Paula made tea, sat down at the kitchen table, and lit a cigarette. It was useless to try to sleep until she had reached some sort of resting point for her mind. The stories haunted her. Lady Hindon's was set in a Gothic mansion, one hundred and fifty years ago. The victim was a ne'er-do-well eldest son of a baronet; the murder-trap was on the steps beside the waterfall in the ornamental gardens. It was hinted, but not proved, that the girl who was to marry the younger son was guilty, and she certainly came to a gruesome end.

The Reverend Rupert Fisher's story was less ambitious but equally effective. It was told in the first person by an insurance salesman who came home after a miserably frustrating day to find his wife dead at the foot of the stairs in their semi-detached suburban house. Crisply written, but full of atmosphere and quiet menace. The reader suspected, early on, that the man himself had set the trap, but the tension was maintained right up to the end.

Paula refilled her teacup and found some digestive biscuits.

Suppose, she said to herself, that I were to set the task of inventing a murder in the home and I wanted very much to make it sound convincing. What would I do? I would look around my home—this kitchen for example—for possibilities of accident until I got an idea. Poisoning? Electrocution? Having decided, I would then experiment with the idea as far as was feasible.

As far as feasible.

That meant avoiding any risk of injury to herself or to anybody else. Putting damp moss onto steep stone steps that somebody was very likely going to walk down in the dark did not come within this category. That was no harmless experiment, but a deliberate attempt to injure.

But in any case, thought Paula, getting up and deciding that she really must try to get some sleep now, it didn't make sense, because the chronology was wrong. You would make your experiment *before* you wrote your story; you would not write the story and then go and test the methods afterwards.

Therefore Frances's accident could not have anything to do with the task she had set her students.

On this conclusion Paula decided to go to bed. She had a suspicion that there were flaws in the reasoning, but she was growing very sleepy, and tomorrow looked like being a strenu-

ous day, so she did her best to blot out all thoughts of booby-
traps in cottage gardens, and to recall to her mind the glory of
the sun setting behind Stonehenge, which had made a great
impression on her, and which she had meant to describe to
Frances—but there had been no opportunity to mention it.

By daybreak the rain had ceased. Paula slept well for several hours and woke to see the slanting sunlight. From her
bedroom window the sloping garden looked innocent and attractive. The rain had brought leaves off the trees, but these
were almost all collected on the level grass at the far end. Very
few had blown onto the steps or the rock garden. In any case,
Paula was quite sure that the moss was to blame.

She washed and dressed quickly, went downstairs and prepared a breakfast tray for Frances, carried it into the front
bedroom and greeted her cheerfully.

"It's a lovely morning."

"I could have got up," protested her friend. "My leg feels
much better."

"Your leg?" Paula pretended to be puzzled. "I thought you
had 'flu."

"Good heavens. I'd almost forgotten. I must have slept
very deeply." Frances looked rather embarrassed. "I don't
think I ought to ask you to do this for me after all. Perhaps I
could pretend that I fell off a stepladder and hurt my ankle."

Paula made no comment. She helped her friend to sit up
comfortably, placed the tray on her lap, and poured the coffee,
one cup each. Then she perched herself on the end of the bed
and spoke.

"I'm very worried about you and I wish you'd be more
open with me."

"Oh, Paula."

"All right. I don't want to hit a woman when she is down.
We won't say any more at the moment. Only that if I'm going
to stay here to help you through the next few days until you
can walk without limping, then I've got to feel free to try to
find out for myself what really happened. That's fair, isn't it?"

"Very fair," said Frances in a low voice, as she sipped her
coffee.

"It would help a lot, though," went on Paula, feeling more
and more mean in the face of her friend's meekness, "to know

whether you have any suspicions, whether you know of anybody who might have a grudge against you."

"The only people who might possibly have a grudge against me," said Frances in a stronger tone, "are not even in England at the moment."

Paula could press it no further. The friendly young neighbours now in Spain, she said to herself as she went downstairs. Were they really so good and kind? But she must not start distrusting everything Frances said. That would create such an intolerable situation between them that their friendship could not survive it. And in any case, she now had the useful admission that there did exist people who might perhaps wish Frances ill.

As is surely the case with all of us, thought Paula as she sat near the kitchen window with a second cup of coffee and a bowl of wheat flakes on the table in front of her. All of us, however quietly we think we live, give offence to somebody or other during the course of our lives, and it's best just not to think about it.

When she finished her breakfast she picked up the piece of moss that she had left lying on the kitchen window-sill the night before, carefully wrapped it in a piece of kitchen paper, and went out into the garden.

Everything was fresh and glistening in sunshine after rain. It seemed a pity, on a lovely morning like this, to be doing this mean and suspicious sort of investigation, but now was her chance.

On the steps where the moss had been there was no sign of any remaining. Just as she had expected. The rain had washed all away. But Paula's main object was the long grass near the apple trees, and her shoes were soaked before she found what she was looking for. Both trees, one a Cox, one a cooking apple, were big and old and spreading and very mossy round the trunk and roots.

Paula leaned down and touched the dark green fronds. It felt cold and rather unpleasant: a sort of sopping sponge. Yesterday it would not have been as wet as this, but quite damp enough, the moss and the earth it grew in.

At the base of both trees there were bare patches, as if

some of the moss might have been torn away. Or perhaps an animal had been scratching there.

Some of the moss had much longer fronds than the other. The specimen that Paula was carrying in the kitchen paper belonged to the shorter type. Or maybe it is all the same, she thought, but some is older than the rest.

For a moment or two she wished that her botanical knowledge was not so scanty, and then she decided that, even in her ignorance, there was a little experiment that she could make. She replaced the vital sample in her jacket pocket and took from the tree-root one piece of the heavier moss and one piece of the shorter. Then she looked around for a suitable slab of stone, placed the mossy earth onto it, then stepped on the stone.

The longer fronds were not particularly slippery. On the contrary, they seemed to provide some sort of grip for the foot. But the other kind, similar to what was in her pocket, formed a good skid-pad. On further exploring this end of the garden, Paula found several places where even a moderately active person could get through the fence, and she marvelled that Frances had not lost all her apples more frequently than on the one occasion she had mentioned.

They must indeed be a very law-abiding village. Or else everybody had too many apples of their own.

Well satisfied with the outcome of her excursion, Paula returned to the house, changed her shoes, put the precious sample of moss at the bottom of her suitcase, and went to knock on the door of Frances's bedroom.

"How goes? Do you need any help?"

"No thanks. I'm coming down in a minute."

"Don't try to carry the tray. I'll fetch it later. I'm going next door to Mrs. Barton. Don't answer the phone or the front door if anybody rings. You're supposed to be ill in bed."

But we're never going to be able to keep that up, thought Paula as she ran downstairs again without waiting for Frances to reply. It was a silly idea, the sort of thing that looks better at night than in the bright light of day. I shall modify it when I talk to the neighbours.

Paula had rather assumed, from Frances's description, that Mrs. Barton would be a nervous little old lady, but the woman who opened the door was tall and elegant in dark red corduroy trousers and jacket, and had thick well-cut grey-blonde hair that was kind to the well-preserved complexion. She looked all set for the taking of photographs advertising clothes or holidays for the older woman, and Paula was conscious that her experiments in the back garden had caused her to look far from well-groomed.

Neither did Mrs. Barton seem to suffer from shyness.

"You must be Frances's clever friend," she said, almost before Paula had stated her name. "I've heard so much about you and was hoping we might meet. Will you be staying for long?"

"It depends on Frances," said Paula, quickly adding, "she's not very well, and I don't want to leave her until she's really better."

"Oh, my dear." The pale blue eyes and pale pink face registered distress. "I'm so sorry. I've never known Frances to be ill. What's the matter with her?"

At this moment Paula found herself developing an intense and quite irrational dislike for Mrs. Barton.

"She's had a bad night and is rather feverish and aching this morning."

Paula hesitated before saying more. She had prepared her story for the mental image of the neighbour, and was not quite sure how to proceed with this very different reality.

Mrs. Barton helped her out. "There's a lot of 'flu about just now. I expect poor Frances has succumbed. Is there anything I can do for her? My husband always used to say that hot lemon and whisky—"

"It's kind of you to offer, but I think the best thing she can do is stay in and keep warm. I'm going to take her class for her this morning and she's promised not to try to do anything."

"I'll drop in and see her then. Later on this morning, when you're out. It will break up the time for her."

Paula stopped herself, just in time, from saying, "No, don't do that."

"That would be very kind," she said instead, "but perhaps it would be as well to telephone first, just to give her warning."

Mrs. Barton agreed, but Paula could see that this remark had not gone down well. The dislike seemed to be mutual. Frances will have to cope with this herself, thought Paula, feeling increasingly irritated with her friend. If all the people she was going to meet turned out to be like Bruce Wiley and Mrs. Barton, then she might as well give up the pretence at once. She was not a good liar and, in any case, it was her belief that in the long run it was better to tell the truth.

"I saw you out very early this morning," said Mrs. Barton, just as Paula was wondering how to get away without giving further offence. "Are you a keen gardener, like Frances?"

"I'm not a gardener at all," replied Paula, wondering with some alarm how much Mrs. Barton had actually seen of her moss experiments. "I just enjoy other people's gardens. And it's lovely to get out into clean fresh air after London."

"We lived in London for some years," said Mrs. Barton, putting on a wistful expression. "In Kensington. Just round at the back of Harrods. That was when my husband was acting as consultant for one of the big hotels."

Paula tried to show polite interest before she said that she really must be going, as she had such a lot to do.

Mrs. Barton took no notice at all, and proceeded with her reminiscences.

In the end Paula was saved by Leslie, who suddenly appeared from nowhere and wound his tail round Paula's ankle and mewed loudly.

"Oh dear, I'd forgotten to feed the cat," exclaimed Paula. "I'll have to go. Goodbye Mrs. Barton. We'll be meeting again."

In Brookside Cottage she found that Frances had come downstairs in her dressing-gown and was sitting at the kitchen table drinking more coffee and reading *The Times*. She looked placid and peaceful, and Paula, feeling flustered and anxious, diverted her annoyance with her friend into making a great fuss of the cat.

"Mrs. Barton wants to come and see you," she said at last.

"Oh, yes. She would."

"I told her she'd better telephone first."

"She might as well come." Frances put down her newspaper and turned to face Paula, who saw then how much the air of calmness had been assumed. "It's not going to work, Paula. Our plan. I'm sorry I suggested it. I was just being cowardly. We'll have to tell people about my fall, but there's no need to mention the moss. They will all believe it was an accident, except perhaps—"

"For the person who put the moss there," said Paula, as Frances seemed reluctant to finish her sentence. "I am so relieved that you've decided to do this," she went on. "I was afraid of letting you down."

"It was too much to ask. What did you think of Mrs. Barton?"

"I don't think we took to each other very much," replied Paula with more caution than she would normally have used, for in spite of what Frances had just said, she still felt that there was a certain degree of distrust between them. "I don't think I would embark on a twice-a-week coffee routine with Mrs. Barton if I lived here."

Frances merely laughed. "She's quite harmless, really."

Paula was not so sure, but she felt that she had been warned off making any suggestion that Mrs. Barton might have been responsible for putting the moss on the steps, and she contented herself with remarking that the neighbour was younger and more active than she had expected.

"Does she do her own gardening?" she asked.

"Unfortunately not. That would have given us a never-ending topic of conversation. She has a young man come in twice a week from further along the valley."

"What's he like?"

"Terry? Tolerably competent." Frances spoke as if she were giving a rather lukewarm school report on a pupil. "He doesn't know much about pruning roses."

"I didn't mean as a gardener," said Paula. "I meant as a person."

"Nondescript," was the prompt reply. "Medium size, medium colouring, quite polite, not very chatty, but that may be policy. Not to offend Mrs. B."

"She's afraid somebody else might steal her treasure from her?"

"She is indeed, though I suspect that somebody else would have to offer very high wages to tempt him away."

Paula would have liked to ask more, for surely Mrs. Barton's gardener was a very suitable person to add to her very meagre list of suspects, but there was no time left. In half an hour she must be at Lady Hindon's, and Frances had to tell her the best way to get there, and wish her luck, and thank her again and again.

Merle House was a solid-looking stone mansion, built in the form of a letter E, with wings at each end forming the top and bottom strokes of the E, and a large covered porch in the centre as the shorter, middle stroke. It was backed by woods, and there were extensive lawns in front.

Paula saw it in slabs of colour: the brilliant green of the grass, the golden-grey of the house, the beech leaves a mixture of copper and green, and the arc of pale blue sky above. As she turned her little yellow car into the drive, between high stone gateposts, she had a momentary impression of a stage back-cloth, two-dimensional, and not a place where people lived and thought and felt.

In front of the house were three cars parked neatly side by side. Paula took trouble to position the mini two feet away from the little red Fiat, telling herself that Merle House was a very orderly place and she must curb her own tendency towards carelessness and untidiness.

As she got out of the car another mini drew up, even older and more battered than her own, and a short stocky grey-haired man got out and came towards her. Rather to Paula's surprise, he introduced himself as Rupert Fisher, retired Unitarian minister, and she found that she had been imagining the author of that grim little murder story to be tall and cadaverous.

She introduced herself and explained about Frances's accident.

"Mrs. Coles phoned Lady Hindon this morning and suggested that I should come along instead," she concluded. "And Lady Hindon agreed. It seemed better than cancelling the class."

"Much better," said Rupert Fisher. "Friday morning is the high spot of my week, you know. And that goes for most of us, including our hostess. How lucky that you were able to take over from Frances. But she is not badly hurt, I hope?"

"Fortunately not. She only needs to rest her ankle for a few days."

"It might have been a very nasty accident," said the Reverend Rupert Fisher thoughtfully.

Paula agreed. All the while that they were talking, she was asking herself whether this cheerful and rather chatty elderly man could possibly have set the booby-trap for Frances. Physically it was possible. He looked active and practical, the sort of man who would go for long walks and maintain his own car. But he certainly did not look in the least like a man who would set a booby-trap for a middle-aged woman; and besides, Paula, though an agnostic, felt unwilling to attribute such deliberate malice to a minister of religion.

"I read your story, Mr. Fisher," she said. "I thought it was very good indeed."

"Did you?" He stopped on the lowest of the four wide, shallow steps that led up to the main entrance of Merle House. "That's—that's very kind."

He looked both eager and embarrassed, and Paula found herself liking him, and hoping she could cross him off her list of suspects. Though why on earth, she asked herself, as a tall white-haired woman opened the door to them, should any of Frances's students want to injure or even to kill her?

"Hullo, Melanie," said Rupert. "This is Miss King," he said to Paula. "Our class secretary."

"Lady Hindon told me about the accident," said Miss King, "and she would like to meet you before we start the class. Would you mind acting as doorkeeper, Rupert?"

"Certainly, ma'am."

Paula was obliged to follow Miss King away from the comforting presence of Rupert Fisher and the sound of other people arriving, across the broad high foyer and along several corridors. The House seemed to her sombre and rather forbidding, but she was becoming too nervous to take in any details of her surroundings.

Frances was right, she said to herself: This is a very hierarchical establishment. And what place did a substitute tutor have in it? Not on a par with the lady of the manor, of course, but did she come above or below the man-of-all-work, Bruce Wiley?; and did he actually live on the premises?; and what position did Miss Melanie King hold?

"Where does the class actually meet?" she asked her companion, feeling that she ought to try out her voice, in case her apprehension should have caused her to lose it altogether.

"In the library," replied Miss King. "We're going there now. Lady Hindon prefers to have coffee before the class, so as not to interrupt the discussion. Mrs. Coles thought this was a good idea too."

"So do I," said Paula. "What about the others?"

"They'll be having theirs in the breakfast room. Usually we all come into the library straight away, but Lady Hindon particularly wanted to speak to you privately this morning. Here we are."

Paula's nervousness built up to a climax as Miss King pushed open the heavy panelled door, but as soon as she entered the room it disappeared completely and did not return again.

"Oh, what a lovely room!" she exclaimed.

The ceiling was high, the far wall was all long windows, with an impression of greenness and blue sky outside. The two side walls were lined with books from floor to ceiling. There was a globe; a large writing desk on which lay books and papers; lots of comfortable chairs; some solid library steps that looked as if they were in frequent use; and a table on which stood the coffee tray and beside which was a wheelchair.

Paula had a shock when she saw the occupant of the chair, not because there was anything in the least bit alarming or repulsive about her, but because there wasn't. Yet again, only half-consciously, she had built up mental image that turned out to be completely false.

From Frances and from Bruce Wiley she had gained the

impression that Lady Hindon, though crippled, was a physically large, commanding-looking woman; but seated in the
wheel-chair was a slight figure wearing a long, light-brown
velvet dress which hid the legs and feet, leaving all attention
to be focussed on the hands, which were still and pale and
beautiful, and on the face, which was equally pale and beautiful within its surround of almost black hair.

Paula had the impression of a Rembrandt portrait, old and
yet ageless, motionless but very much alive.

"Dr. Glenning?" The woman in the wheelchair held out
one of the lovely hands. "How very kind of you to come to
our rescue. Do sit down. Would you mind looking after the
others, please, Miss King? Give us ten minutes. It has only
just gone twenty past ten."

All three of them glanced at the grandfather clock that
stood to the right of the library door. It was a large and stately
plain-faced clock, which suited its surroundings, and Paula
had no doubt that it kept perfect time.

Paula took an upright chair at the side of the table, a few
feet away from Lady Hindon, accepted a cup of coffee, and
awaited the interrogation. Her friendship with Frances, her
own position, the accident—all were touched on with such
calm politeness that there was no possibility of taking offence.
Paula was immensely relieved that, except in one particular,
she had only to tell the truth.

"It is fortunate," said Lady Hindon, "that Mrs. Coles was
not more seriously hurt. I have never seen her garden, but I
understand from Mr. Wiley that the steps are very steep."

"Yes indeed. I am always very careful when I use them
myself."

"And one must assume that your friend is careful too. She
is by no means a careless and impulsive sort of person. However." Lady Hindon smiled faintly. "Such accidents are happening all the time. Many of them must remain unaccounted
for. In real life, I mean. In fiction, of course, we demand and
are entitled to receive explanations. Did you have time to read
my story, Dr. Glenning?"

"I did indeed, Lady Hindon, and I was most impressed by
it. I thought the recreation of the period, and the sense of
menace, were very good indeed."

Lady Hindon smiled again, but said nothing.

Mona Lisa, thought Paula suddenly. Not a Rembrandt, but Leonardo's eternally enigmatic woman, if one could imagine her grown old. And equally suddenly came the thought: How did she lose the use of her legs? Was it an accident? Was the short story perhaps based on her own life story?

"Where would you like to sit?" asked Lady Hindon. "Mrs. Coles prefers to sit at the table, and the students place themselves in a semicircle. It is all quite informal, as you see."

"I should like to do the same as Mrs. Coles," said Paula.

It was rather like training to teach, she thought as she arranged her papers on the table in front of her. Lady Hindon would make an excellent supervisor for a learner-teacher. Curiously enough, Paula did not feel in the least bit nervous. There was something rather comforting about Lady Hindon's assumption of complete authority. It was as if you were her creature, her possession, and while you served her she would support you faithfully and protect you against all-comers, in the same way a devoted cat-owner will defend her pet.

My servant, right or wrong. It was indeed very feudal, in the true sense of the word. Could it possibly be that Frances herself had offended in some way and put herself outside the pale of the benevolent despotism? Was the booby-trap on the steps meant to teach her a lesson? Of course Lady Hindon could not possibly have put the moss there herself, but her right-hand man could have done it for her.

Bruce Wiley came into the library last of all, watched for a moment while the others seated themselves, and then shut the door.

"Mrs. Long and Mrs. Findlay have sent their apologies," he said, sitting down on an upright chair near to the door. "Mrs. Long is not well, and Mrs. Findlay has an unexpected visit from her daughter."

Paula watched him as he spoke, hoping to discover some hint of the relationship between him and his employer, but apart from the fact that he appeared to comply willingly with the Merle House rules of formality, she could detect nothing.

"Thank you, Mr. Wiley," said Lady Hindon. "Then we need not delay any longer. You will all know by now that Mrs. Coles has had an accident, fortunately not very serious, and that her friend Dr. Paula Glenning of the University of London has kindly consented to lead our seminar this morning. Dr.

Glenning." She turned to face Paula. "I must introduce the members of our group to you. Miss Melanie King, on your right, you have already met. Mr. Bruce Wiley likewise. Next to him is Mrs. Jill Freebody."

She paused for a second or two while Paula smiled at a small fair woman wearing very large-rimmed glasses.

"Mrs. Gloria Alexander."

A broad, tweedy-looking woman whom Paula learned later shared a house with Mrs. Freebody, beamed and nodded at Paula.

"Mr. Rupert Fisher."

"We met on the doorstep," said Paula.

"Mr. Norman Smith."

Paula's eyes turned to a middle-aged man who looked as if he might be a farmer.

"Mr. Ernest Brooker."

This last-named was seated a few feet away from Lady Hindon, with his back to the window. He was thin, white haired, and had a sad, scholarly face. Paula had the impression that not only was he the oldest of the group, but that Lady Hindon's voice softened slightly as she turned to him.

"Good morning, Dr. Glenning. We are all most grateful to you."

He spoke very formally, and Paula noted that he had an exceptionally beautiful voice.

"Good morning," said Paula, adding to herself that she was not mistaken; that there was definitely a suggestion of preferential treatment for Mr. Ernest Brooker. A personal friend of Lady Hindon, perhaps?

Later on she might learn more. At the moment she was very fully occupied in trying to fix the names in her mind.

Lady Hindon shifted her wheelchair away from the table where Paula sat, positioned herself next to Mr. Brooker, clasped the beautiful hands lightly together, and let them rest against the brown velvet of her dress. She said no more, but her gestures said clearly to Paula that she was abdicating her position as hostess and was from now on simply a student like the others.

Paula had intended to make a little opening speech, saying that she was pleased to meet them all and hoping that they would excuse her deficiencies, since her experience was entirely with university students and not with adult students from a variety of backgrounds; but she decided to leave this out. Lady Hindon, though exceedingly formal, obviously did not like unnecessary speeches. Economy of word, thought, and gesture—that seemed to be her guiding principle. Very well, then; let it provide the theme for this meeting.

"What struck me most about the short stories you have written," she said, glancing round the circle and plunging straight in without preamble, "is the economy of the writing. Here is an example of what I mean."

From the pile of scripts on the table in front of her she pulled out one at random: a handwritten script, in clear forward-sloping writing.

"'Jemima Wheatley had been forty for three months and was not liking it at all,'" she read aloud. "That's just right for an opening sentence," she continued. "A short sentence, only"—she paused a moment—"fifteen words. Let's analyse it, shall we, and see just how much information is contained in that one sentence, which also, incidentally, sets the tone for the whole story."

She looked round again. There was no doubt that she had gripped her audience. Among the interested faces there was one that seem to be even more beaming than the rest. It was the little fair woman with the big glasses who sat next to the big tweedy woman. Mrs. Gloria Alexander. No. That was tweedy herself. Paula surreptitiously glanced at her list. Mrs. Jill Freebody was the fair one. Forty? Probably.

"It's your story, isn't it, Mrs. Freebody?" she said. "It illustrates the point I am making. And so do all the others. Economy of writing. A sure and speedy effect that holds the reader. Yes, Mr. Smith?"

The "farmer" who sat between the Reverend Rupert Fisher and Mr. Ernest Brooker looked as if he wanted to speak.

"That sentence," he began rather hesitantly after a quick look in the direction of Lady Hindon, "gives us the name and age of the character and tells us something about her. She doesn't want to grow old."

"Very true," said Paula. "We get a suggestion of a character. What sort of suggestion do we get?"

Several people began to speak at once. Paula, sorting out priorities, also looked towards Lady Hindon for a moment and saw on that aged Mona Lisa face an alert and attentive smile very different from that in the portrait.

There was no doubt that, as a teacher, she had gained Lady Hindon's approval, and that the class was going to be a success.

# 5

Mrs. Gloria Alexander was giving her opinion. She had a clear strong voice and was making sensible, though not very original, remarks about the difficulty of establishing a character within the limits of a short story.

Paula, temporarily released from the need to speak, decided that Mrs. Alexander had been a schoolteacher. An imperial-sounding name, an imperious personality. What was the relationship between her and the little fair woman, twenty-five years her junior, with whom she shared a house? The differences in age and physique were not unlike those between Paula and Frances. There would be no doubt plenty of tensions in such a ménage. Which was the dominant character, wondered Paula.

In Mrs. Alexander's short story the murderer was a woman, a poor downtrodden creature who poisoned her bullying husband. It was a competent enough piece of writing, but not up to the standard of most of the others. Maybe Mrs. Alexander only came to the classes in order to be with her more gifted friend.

"Thank you," said Paula as soon as she could see a chance to interrupt, for Mrs. Alexander had talked long enough. "Can we think of any other ways of overcoming this problem?"

"It is simplest, perhaps," said Mr. Brooker in the voice that was a pleasure to listen to, "to tell the story in the first

35

person so that the reader sees through the eyes of that person."

"As you did yourself," said Paula. "And Mr. Fisher. And Mrs. Alexander and Mr. Wiley, and Mrs. Freebody. More than half the class chose this solution. And it is also interesting—"

She paused for a moment, wondering if what she was about to say was too personal, perhaps too suggestive, but finally deciding that they all needed a little light relief after Mrs. Gloria Alexander's speech, which had brought a slight sense of oppression into the atmosphere.

"Interesting, isn't it," she continued with a smile, "that in all these cases of a narrator-murderer, the victim was the spouse."

She glanced round the circle of faces. They were all smiling too; the joke had come off. Even the thin, sombre face of Mr. Ernest Brooker showed a hint of amusement, and Rupert Fisher and Norman Smith were openly laughing.

"The Hercule Poirot touch," said Bruce Wiley. "Do we now await the confession of the one who really did it, Dr. Glenning?"

"We are talking about the technique of creating suspense in fiction," said Paula with mock severity, looking straight at him and receiving a mocking glance in return. "All writing is, in a sense, a sort of self-revelation," she continued, addressing the whole group, "but if anybody has any specific confession to make, perhaps he or she will postpone it to a more suitable occasion. I am sure Lady Hindon will agree."

Lady Hindon nodded without speaking. She too was smiling, but Paula suspected that there was malice mixed with the amusement, and she rather wished now that she had never made that remark about the narrator-murderer and the spouse as victim.

Frances, experienced in teaching creative writing to adults, would never have done so. Frances would have known that there was an unspoken agreement between the tutor and the members of the class that must always be respected. Of course people wrote from their own experience or from their own fantasy; everybody knew that. But, equally of course, when discussing the art of writing, you never openly referred to this fact; you confined yourself to discussing the product, not the author.

Paula, accustomed to detailed examination of the lives and thoughts of the great writers, had forgotten for the moment that in a little group of amateurs, you did not analyse the motives behind the writing of the fiction. You kept your thoughts and suspicions about the author to yourself.

She had broken the rule. The class all knew it, but their smiles showed that they forgave her. Even Bruce Wiley, whose intervention seen in this light could be taken as a broad hint to get back onto the right track, was not going to refer to it again, although he and Lady Hindon would perhaps talk about it afterwards.

Or perhaps not. Paula had the impression that Lady Hindon had enjoyed the remark and would have liked the discussion to continue along more personal lines, with other people getting increasingly involved, but without speaking herself. A crippled old lady. Very intelligent, a lover of power. Wielding great authority through her wealth and position, but personally very helpless. It was quite likely that she enjoyed the revelation of people's frailties, but would she actually confide her thoughts to anybody? On the whole, Paula thought not.

All this was going through her mind as she asked Miss Melanie King, who had not as yet spoken, if she would agree to read her own story aloud so that the class could do a detailed analysis.

Paula chose Miss King because she had written the most mild and gentle of the stories. It was about a mercy-killing, the overdosing of a dying much-suffering mother by a devoted daughter. The story was told through the voice of the family doctor; the suspense lay in his suspicions and his dilemma. Should he tell the truth?

It was a moving little tale and Paula was convinced that it had been written from personal experience.

Miss Melanie King read it in a clear voice that betrayed little emotion. If this was indeed her own tragedy, she had herself well under control. When she had finished there was a murmur of appreciation from the class.

Mrs. Gloria Alexander's voice came out loudest.

"Well, I think the doctor was quite right to tell the police. After all, killing is killing."

Mr. Smith, Mr. Brooker, and Mr. Fisher all spoke at once,

disagreeing with her, Rupert Fisher being the most determined to be heard.

"The doctor ought to have kept quiet. There had been suffering enough."

Nice man, thought Paula, as others began to join in the argument.

"The story certainly makes its point," she said loudly, interrupting them. "Otherwise it would not arouse such controversy. But we are not here to decide on morals. We are here to discuss whether a piece of writing is effective or not. Does anybody have anything to say on this?"

"Yes," said Lady Hindon, speaking for the first time. "In my opinion this story meets the requirements of economy and simplicity. It is very much to the point and there is no padding. I like it."

She turned to look at Miss King. Paula turned too, and saw the white-haired lady flush slightly and appear to be very occupied with her papers.

"I like it too," said Paula. "Any other comments?"

Mr. Brooker thought it was perhaps almost too economical: The character of the doctor could have been more fully developed, thus heightening the interest of the reader in his dilemma.

Nobody else agreed with him. Was this their genuine opinion, wondered Paula, or did they all hesitate to differ from Lady Hindon? If indeed her word were law, or, as in this instance, literary judgment, then it was just as well that she did not utter many words. In fact she made no further contribution to the discussion, which continued to be both lively and amicable until the two hours were over.

Paula was almost sorry when the grandfather clock struck half past midday. She felt that she was getting the feel of this sort of teaching and was rather enjoying herself. She also felt that, in spite of the formal atmosphere and the conformity to unspoken laws, she was actually learning quite a lot about the people present.

Mr. Brooker's position as a privileged friend of the hostess was definitely established, and so too was Lady Hindon's protective attitude towards Miss King.

That most people had to exercise their forbearance in the case of Mrs. Alexander was also evident; so too was the fact that the universal awe of Lady Hindon extended in some degree towards her henchman, Bruce Wiley.

Mr. Norman Smith and Mr. Rupert Fisher were obviously old friends. Both seemed to be good-hearted, open characters. Mrs. Jill Freebody, who had written the story about the woman who hated being forty, was, in Paula's opinion, the least self-revealing in the group.

It was impossible to guess at her real opinion of her overbearing housemate, Mrs. Alexander, and Paula noticed that it was actually Jill Freebody who drove the Mercedes in which the two of them departed. A paid companion? A poor relation?

Lady Hindon, propelling her own chair, came into the front hall of Merle House to wish them all goodbye. Bruce Wiley walked protectively beside her. Mr. Brooker and Miss King remained in the library. Apparently they had been asked to stay for lunch. Paula wondered who would prepare it. She had seen no sign of any housekeeper or other staff during the whole morning.

A glance from Bruce Wiley told Paula not to depart until Mr. Smith and Mr. Fisher had driven off in their noisy little cars. Paula was disappointed; she would have liked to speak to Rupert Fisher again.

Bruce Wiley disappeared and Paula found herself once more alone with Lady Hindon.

"Thank you very much, Dr. Glenning," she said, "for a most instructive and entertaining session. The little—" she paused almost imperceptibly—"indiscretion was most effective, was it not?"

Paula, feeling quite unequal to a verbal battle of subtleties and innuendo, burst out with what she really felt.

"Oh, Lady Hindon, I'm so sorry I made that stupid remark about narrator-murderers! I do hope I haven't offended anybody."

"You certainly haven't offended me." The Mona Lisa smile broadened. "On the contrary. It had the makings of a very interesting situation. As Mr. Wiley said, the denouement of a classic closed-circle detective story. Did you notice the reactions?"

"Everybody seemed to be amused," said Paula.

"Possibly. Possibly not everybody," was the cryptic reply.

"Amusement can be faked, perhaps more easily than other emotions. But I must not keep you, Dr. Glenning. You will be anxious to return to your friend. How long do you propose to remain with her?"

"Certainly over the weekend. Perhaps until Tuesday or Wednesday."

"In that case we may meet again. If she is equal to the exertion, I should very much like to see her. Could you bring her to tea on Sunday?"

Paula, very much taken aback, said she would gladly drive Frances over to Merle House.

"Four o'clock," said Lady Hindon. "Goodbye. My regards to Mrs. Coles."

Paula drove back along the pretty winding lane to Winsford with her mind full of Lady Hindon and the rest of Frances's students, and longing to talk to Frances about them. But, as on the previous evening, this happy anticipation was not to be fulfilled. As she turned the corner into the side road just short of the Shepherd's Rest, she saw that the place outside Frances's garage where her mini had stood was occupied by another car, a pale blue Vauxhall with a big dent in the side.

Paula felt a spurt of irritation, first because she did not want to share Frances with any other visitor just at this moment, and second, because there was no other space available, except that reserved for customers at the inn. Reluctantly, for she was a conscientious and considerate motorist, she turned into the yard of the Shepherd's Rest, found a space, and was just walking back across the lane when a young man caught up with her.

"You must be Paula."

"That's my name," said Paula in no very friendly tones. "What's yours?"

"Andrew Melville Coles. My mama said you liked a dry Riesling, so I hope this will do." He made a little flourish with the bottle he was carrying. "She also told me to get my car out of the way before you arrived, but since you are safely at rest with the Shepherd, and I am a customer of his . . ."

"Then that point is covered too," said Paula, still quite sharply.

Frances's son looked like so many of the students at the Princess Elizabeth College where she taught: healthy, lively, and aimless. In her more gloomy moments, Paula sometimes thought of them as a lost generation, these boys and girls of today, who had grown up to believe that so much was open to them, and had inherited a shrunken, tortured, and half-crazy world.

"When did you get here?" she asked, rather more amicably.

For Frances's sake, for the sake of all three of them, she and Andrew Coles must modify their instant mutual antipathy.

"About half an hour ago. Since when my mother has been lecturing me on how I ought to behave towards you. I don't know whether I'm doing it right. I'm usually in the wrong, as far as Mama is concerned."

A fair, good-looking face—much less reserved than that of his mother. Paula's dislike became tinged with sympathy. After all, she herself knew nothing of Frances in her capacity as wife and mother. Frances was a tough character; strong emotions were held tautly in check. Maybe she had been over-possessive, overdemanding. Maybe both husband and son, unable to live up to her high expectations, had sunk into a sort of grumbling apathy.

They approached the door of Brookside Cottage, Paula with the fear that she was going to be drawn straight into the family tension, and Andrew talking about his mother's accident.

"I knew she'd come walloping down those steps one day, but of course you can't tell her. Mother knows best. Always."

This is going to be awful, thought Paula. Frances is going to nag him and I am going to bend over backwards finding excuses for him.

But in fact it did not turn out so badly after all. Just as a pet cat or dog is an invaluable focus of attention and conversation for people who have nothing to say to each other, so a sprained ankle can be a useful diversion for people who have too much to say.

Frances was hobbling around her kitchen, putting knives and plates on the table. Paula and Andrew, in unspoken agreement, urged her to sit down, took cheese and cold meats from the fridge, and for the best part of ten minutes continued to talk about nothing but the preparation of the meal.

After a halfhearted attempt to rearrange their table setting,

Frances left them to it and contented herself with sitting down and giving instructions.

She ate very little, but Paula and Andrew were both hungry, and praised the cheese and the wine.

Frances turned to Andrew. "Did you move your car to let Paula in?"

"He was going to," said Paula before Andrew could speak, "but there's plenty of space in the car-park at the pub."

Andrew glanced at her gratefully and Paula immediately felt misgivings. She had not intended so openly to take his side.

"But I'd better shift it before this evening," she added. "They seem to get very full up then. I can leave it further up the lane."

"You'll do no such thing." Frances's voice was that of the ruler of the classroom. "Andrew will move his car. That is, if he proposes to stay here. He'll have to sleep in the boxroom."

To Paula's great relief Andrew said he would not be staying overnight. "This guy in Salisbury will give me a bed," he added. "The one I was telling you about."

"The used-car dealer," said Frances contemptuously. "I would not have thought that a good history degree was a qualification for dealing in stolen cars."

"Why not?" said Andrew. "They both require a certain reappraisal of the past."

So that's it, thought Paula, as mother and son settled down to their argument. Clever boy rebels against parent's ambitions for him and won't do a proper job. It happened again and again with her own students. A great pity, but in these days of high unemployment it was so common that it was not worth breaking one's heart over. If that was all that was wrong with Andrew, then Frances really didn't have all that cause to complain.

But was that all? Paula, getting up from the table to make coffee, wondered whether perhaps the mother and son were now in league together, rolling out the old familiar arguments for the benefit of the outsider, in order to conceal the much deeper layer of tension between them.

The telephone ring was a welcome diversion.

"I'll get it," said Andrew.

They heard him in the hall, saying that yes, Mrs. Coles was there, but not able . . .

"I'm awfully sorry about this, Paula," said Frances stiffly.

"About what?"

Paula heard her own voice as bright and insincere. Then, suddenly afraid that her happy friendship with her former teacher might be slipping away forever, she made a great effort to restore confidence between them. "What would you like me to do, Frances? If you would rather I go back to London now, so that Andrew and you can talk in peace, or if you'd like me to go out for the afternoon—"

"Oh, no. Don't go!"

Frances actually stretched out a hand towards her in her agitation. Paula took it and held it tightly for a moment as she saw the fear and the pleading in her friend's face. Nothing was said, but there was no need for words—it was a promise.

"Very persistent female," said Andrew, coming back into the kitchen. "Won't leave a message. Wants to talk to you or Paula, Mama."

"But who is it?"

"Oh. Didn't I say?" Andrew was standing by the window, looking down the garden. "Mrs. Alexander."

"I'll talk to her," said Paula.

Andrew had left the receiver lying on the hall table. It occurred to Paula that the voice at the other end of the wire had probably not stopped at all.

"—but won't keep her a moment," it was saying.

Paula announced herself and resigned herself to hearing it all over again. Gloria Alexander turned out to be a compulsive talker, and it spoke volumes for the force of Lady Hindon's character that the writing class was only very occasionally subjected to one of her monologues.

The object of the present call was to invite Frances—and Paula too, of course—to go for a drive and to have tea in Salisbury.

"The most gorgeous cream cakes," said Gloria. "They've only been open a few weeks and Jill and I go every Friday. Frances won't have to walk any distance at all. You can't park there, of course, because it's right in the middle of town, just a stone's throw from the cathedral, but we can stop to let Frances out, and the manager is a delightful young man—

he'll find us a comfortable table—and I'm sure it will do
Frances all the good in the world to get out for a while,
and—"

"I'll ask her," said Paula, making herself heard at last, "but
I doubt if she will be able to accept. She has visitors here at
the moment."

Had it escaped Gloria's notice that a male voice had answered the phone, she wondered.

Apparently not. "Oh yes," said Gloria immediately, "but
Andrew is just about to leave. He said so himself."

Paula was rather taken aback. Frances's son had up till now
been to her some sort of shadowy mystery; but apparently his
comings and goings were a matter of course to Gloria Alexander. Yet again she realised just how little she knew of
Frances's life.

"Hold on," she said into the telephone, and put it down
while Gloria was still talking.

At that moment the front door bell rang, and Paula opened
it to let in the neighbour, Mrs. Barton.

"Andrew is here," she said to Paula. "I saw his car and I
thought Frances might like some support."

Paula was intrigued by this remark, but unfortunately it
was not possible to follow it up at this moment. Frances had to
be told of Gloria's invitation, and after a short discussion it
was decided that Paula should accept for herself alone. At
least, she thought as she said goodbye to the others, I ought to
find out some more about Gloria Alexander and Jill Freebody.

It was sad to leave poor Frances to the mercy of Andrew
and Mrs. Barton, but presumably this sort of situation had
arisen before, and surely Frances could come to no harm, with
the two of them there.

So Paula argued with herself, but nevertheless she felt uneasy.

## — 6 —

To Paula's great relief, she was allowed to sit in the back of the Mercedes beside a friendly and well-behaved King Charles spaniel. Gloria sat beside Jill Freebody, who was driving, and the shape of the headrest on the front seat made it difficult for her to turn and talk to Paula, although she did her best.

"I wonder if we ought to pop in and see Frances for a moment," she said as she got in.

"I really don't think—" began Paula politely, but Jill settled the matter by simply driving away.

Gloria turned her head as far as she was able.

"I hope you don't mind dogs, Paula, but we'd had to leave Timmy at home all morning because Lady Hindon doesn't like him in the house, and she also says she can't bear to think of him shut up in the car, although he doesn't mind a bit, he's a good boy, isn't he?—and he loves going for a drive, and—"

Paula was perfectly contented with her travelling companion, who was now sitting up and looking out of the window.

"He's fine," she said, "and so am I. It was very kind of you to come and collect me."

"Oh, we didn't go out of our way. We're only a mile out of Winsford in the direction of Stonehenge."

"Then I must have passed your house last evening," said Paula. "I didn't realise you lived so near to Frances."

"Oh, my dear, we're always asking if we can collect her

45

and bring her home on Friday mornings to save her the drive, but she always says no."

"She likes to drive on her own to collect her thoughts before the class," said Jill.

"Well, I'm sure we wouldn't disturb her," said Gloria, rather huffily.

Jill did not respond, and Gloria did not speak again for a full half-minute. If they had been alone, thought Paula, they'd probably be having a little quarrel now, and she felt that her question had been answered: In this partnership it was the quiet little Mrs. Freebody, inscrutable behind her large spectacles, who had the last word.

The forty-five-minute tour of local beauty spots bore out this judgment. Jill was an excellent driver and the car very comfortable. Paula leaned back, fondled the silky ears of the little brown and white spaniel, and several times shut her eyes. Gloria's voice informed her that the house over there on the hill was the home of a famous television personality, or that they were just passing a tiny thatched cottage that had sold for a quarter of a million pounds.

"Really?" murmured Paula, scarcely troubling to open her eyes. She was very tired after the exertions of the last twenty-four hours, and grateful for this unexpected chance to relax.

"You can see Salisbury Cathedral from here."

Paula heard Gloria's words as in a dream. For a moment or two she had actually been asleep.

"What about Timmy?" she asked as they came into the city. "Is he allowed into the cake-shop?"

Jill answered. "Yes. He's very good. And as we haven't got Frances to consider, we'll go straight to the car-park."

Expertly she reversed the Mercedes into the one of the few remaining vacancies, while Gloria fussed and said there was not going to be enough room. Paula found herself becoming more and more curious about Jill. What was her history? Why did she put up with Gloria? And did Gloria herself realise just how much Jill despised her?

Over tea, thought Paula, she must try to find the answers to some of these questions. Otherwise it would be a wasted afternoon.

She would have liked to linger for a while on the bridge over the little stream, where yellow leaves were floating on dark water, with mellowed brick houses beyond, and a glimpse of the slender spire above them, but both Gloria and Jill were apparently eager for their pastries.

They sat in a little alcove by a window, on thickly cushioned high-backed chairs, Paula next to Gloria, with Jill the other side of the table. On the fourth seat the little dog curled up and surveyed the three of them with loving sentimental brown eyes.

A rosy-faced girl dressed in pale blue took their order. Paula, not at all hungry, asked for the plainest of the cakes. Jill and Gloria chose the most luscious. At least that was one thing they had in common, thought Paula.

"Well, what do you really think of us all?" asked Jill when the rosy girl had gone.

"Think of you?" Paula was taken aback. "You mean the writing class?"

"The writing class. That ill-assorted collection of fumbling amateurs."

There was a smile on the lips of the little woman, but aggression in the voice.

"Amateurs, well yes," said Paula. "You wouldn't expect professional writers to come to such a class. I don't know about fumbling. I was surprised how good the stories were, but then I haven't any experience of this sort of teaching."

"That was moderately obvious."

The smile remained, the aggression intensified.

"Jill, dear," said Gloria, who had been looking from one to the other of them with an expression of alarm on her plump pink face, "don't you think that—"

"I ought not to have made that remark about the murder of a spouse," said Paula, controlling her own rising irritation with some difficulty. "Lady Hindon herself ticked me off about it. Very courteously, of course."

"Of course. Lady Hindon is the soul of courtesy."

At this moment the tea and cakes arived, but as soon as the rosy girl had gone, Jill Freebody returned to her theme.

"I suppose you realise what the purpose of the class really is?"

"For people interested in writing to improve their skills, I suppose," said Paula.

Jill laughed, so suddenly and so harshly that it startled

Gloria into dropping a glob of whipped cream on the table cloth. Against the background of her protests, Jill spoke again.

"If that's all they wanted, there are several good classes in Salisbury, and it's not all that much further to drive for most of us. Would you like me to tell you exactly why we are all there? I'm sure you are bursting with curiosity, aren't you?"

"I don't think, Jill—" began Gloria.

She still looked worried. Her confident chatter seemed to have dried up, and she seemed almost to be shrinking, like a punctured air balloon.

"Yes, tell me," said Paula, addressing Jill. "Of course I'm interested. The whole setup seems to be rather unusual, but I've had very little chance to talk to Frances about it yet, what with one thing and another."

"And she wouldn't have told you if you had. Right. Let's start with the least interesting of the members. The genuine ones who have come to learn to write, and since all people are snobs at heart, enjoy the idea of going to a class at Lady Hindon's country estate. There are four in this category. The two absentees, plus the old parson and his farmer friend. I don't think they've got any guilty secrets, or if they have, they're not relevant."

"Guilty secrets?" Paula could not help but be intrigued. Was she about to hear something that might approximate the truth, or was Jill Freebody about to tell her another fiction?

"Eliminating those four," continued Jill, "and also Gloria and myself for the present, we are left with Ernest, Melanie, Bruce, and Lady Hindon herself. God knows what sins her ladyship has committed in the past. She was a ballet dancer, you know. Also a very efficient gold-digger. The late Sir Reginald was her third husband, and the richest. He died in a plane crash, so we can't include her among the possible spouse-murderers."

"Nor Melanie King," interposed Paula sharply, "since she is not married."

"Nor Melanie King," agreed Jill. "Her pathetic little drama was of another kind."

"You mean the story she wrote was a true one?"

"In essentials. The hopeless invalid was an older sister. They were both nurses. Well known in the area."

"But surely she would not have written that story if she thought there was any risk," protested Paula.

"There was no risk. The inquest on Norma King exonerated her completely. Suicide of a desperately ill woman. Cartloads of flowers and sympathy from grateful ex-patients and pitying acquaintances. Particularly Lady Hindon herself. And grateful Melanie will lick her shoes. And of course she'd taken the chance to make her little confession. As she was expected to do. As we were all expected to do."

Gloria, abandoning all attempts to silence her friend, sighed hugely and took another éclair. Opposite her, Timmy, now curled up on the seat, gave a little whine as if he had been dreaming, and resettled himself in a new position.

"Do you mean," said Paula, putting down her teacup, "that Lady Hindon asked Frances to set this particular assignment in the hope that members of the class might reveal something of their own histories in the stories they wrote on the theme of a murder in the home?"

"You've got it," said Jill, picking up a fork with which to attack her meringue.

"But why? It sounds crazy. Not to say rather dangerous."

"Lady Hindon has a power complex. And she just loves to stir up trouble."

This, at least, Paula found easy to believe.

"But just a minute," she said. "Even if she was hoping that people might give themselves away, what reason did she have to suspect that anybody had any particular guilty secret to come out? Except in the case of Miss King, but as you describe it, that might almost be doing her a kindness, giving her the opportunity to ease her conscience rather than exposing her to suspicion."

"She had reason to suspect," said Jill, "because she had deliberately asked the people concerned to attend the class."

"Oh, really. This is too farfetched." Paula took another apple doughnut. It was quite true that the cakes here were excellent. "And absurdly complicated," she went on. "If one wanted to show one's power over somebody whom one suspected of having a guilty secret, surely there are better ways of doing it than obliging them to attend a writing class and then giving them an embarrassing assignment to write."

"Such as? Remember that there is no question of blackmail

involved here. The object is to torment the victim. What ways
do you suggest?"

"Oh, I don't know," said Paula irritably. "Anonymous letters, perhaps."

"Totally out of character, and insufficient opportunity to
observe the effect."

"Subtle hints in public, then."

"That's more like it. They will follow next week, when our
two absentees return, and Frances is back to play her part. The
people in question will be asked to read their stories aloud,
and the hints will begin. Not that today was wasted. It wasn't
quite what was intended, but you succeeded admirably in
creating a suitable effect."

"I still say it's absurd," said Paula, glancing at Gloria, who
was eating yet another cake, a miserable expression on her
face. "If anybody really had committed a crime, the last thing
they would do would be to use that sort of crime as the subject
of their short story."

"Maybe, but maybe in the very conscious avoidance of it
they might still give themselves away."

"So what are these crimes supposed to be? Who have we
got left, besides Miss King? There's Mr. Brooker."

"Yes. He's a possibility," said Jill.

"And Bruce Wiley."

"Another candidate."

"And, of course, your two selves."

Gloria choked on a crumb and had a coughing fit. Jill at-
tended to her most solicitously. When she had recovered,
Gloria said with more dignity than Paula would have expected
of her, "I think this joke has gone far enough, Jilly dear. Paula
will begin to believe you if you don't stop now. Jill was my
late husband's secretary," she explained to Paula. "She's
always been a great practical joker and a bit of a tease. You
mustn't take her seriously. Writing mystery stories is just up
her street. It's perfectly true that Lady Hindon does enjoy
gloating over people's weaknesses, and that Melanie perhaps
did attempt to shorten her poor sister's sufferings, but as far as
the rest of us are concerned, well, as you said yourself, it's
quite absurd."

Oddly enough, it was this statement of Gloria's, rather than
Jill's malicious suggestions, that convinced Paula that there

was some truth in the latter. She felt now that she ought to change the subject, or suggest that it was time to get back to Frances, but in fact she very much wanted to hear more.

Jill, unprompted, obliged her.

"I may have exaggerated a little," she admitted. "It's possible that Lady Hindon had nothing specific in mind, but just wanted to stir things up in the hope of creating mischief. I'm sure Frances knew what Lady Hindon was after, and didn't like it at all, but could not see a way to get out of it. In fact I shouldn't be surprised if Frances didn't have that accident on purpose when she knew you were coming, so as to have an excuse to get out of today's class."

Paula was just about to protest strongly at what seemed to be a totally unwarranted reflection on her friend, when it suddenly struck her that maybe it was not so preposterous after all. Had she not herself, from the very first, felt there was something odd about Frances's fall?

It struck her now, what in all her investigations she had managed to avoid seeing, that Frances, though refusing to see a doctor, was in fact making more of her own injuries than they warranted. This was totally out of character. Frances was the sort of woman who dealt with minor ailments by ignoring them. If Paula had not been there, and she had such a fall, she would have picked herself up and gone about her business with a limp and feeling rather bruised, but she would certainly not have declared herself out of action.

Jill Freebody's explanation of the accident seemed to Paula most unpleasantly convincing. Frances had been making use of Paula, even perhaps planting a false clue—the moss—to heighten the appearance of mystery that Paula always found irresistible. Was such deviousness out of character too? The Frances whom Paula had known would not have done this; but then the Frances whom Paula had known seemed to be turning out to be the tip of the iceberg.

"I see you are impressed by my theory," said Jill, watching Paula closely. "Hadn't it occurred to you that Frances wanted to avoid today's meeting?"

"Of course it had," said Paula stiffly. "We actually discussed it."

Jill looked as if she didn't believe her, but said no more on the subject of Paula's friend. She had sown her seed of doubt in Paula's mind, and was leaving it to do its own work. Instead she said, turning to look at Gloria, "Are you all right? Have you got your pills?"

Gloria's high colour had faded to a smudgy grey; her mouth was open and her whole body was sagging.

"I've had one," she muttered. "Better in a moment."

"Angina," explained Jill to Paula. "The attacks don't last long. Sorry, old thing," she added when Gloria began to regain her colour. "Maybe I did let the joke go too far."

Gloria took a deep breath, opened her purse and took out two ten-pound notes, picked up the bill, and prepared to rise from her seat.

"Will you bring Timmy, please," she said to Jill. And then, just before getting up, she added in a calm, sad voice quite unlike her usual manner, "Yes, I think you have let the joke go too far."

They walked back to the car-park in silence, Jill carrying the little dog across the busy road, Paula carrying the packet of shortbread that Gloria had bought, and wondering whether she could possibly make some excuse to stay in Salisbury by herself for a while and then return to Winsford by bus or taxi.

She was aching to be alone, but could think of nothing that would sound convincing.

"I suppose there isn't time for a look at the cathedral," she said tentatively.

"Gloria is too tired," replied Jill, "and I've seen it dozens of times, but we can wait for you provided you're not too long."

Paula felt obliged to reject this halfhearted offer, although she was very tempted—so great was her disinclination for the drive back—to accept it and then just disappear.

Even the little spaniel seemed to be affected by the prevailing heaviness of spirit. Instead of sitting up eagerly at the window as the car moved off, he crouched down beside Paula and laid his head on her lap.

For the first mile or two no word was spoken. Then Gloria, turning round as far as she was able, said, "I do hope, Paula, that you will try to forget all this nonsense of Jill's. And not worry Frances with it. She's got trouble enough with Andrew. If only he would settle down to a proper job."

"Perhaps she worries too much about him," said Paula

soothingly. "Lots of young people go through this sort of rest-less period."

"He's not all that young," said Jill. "Twenty-seven."

Again there was silence in the car.

"I ought to have explained, Paula," said Jill presently, "how Gloria and I came to set up house together. I'm sure you're dying to know. It's all right, old girl." She took a hand off the steering-wheel for a moment to touch Gloria's arm. "This is going to be purely factual. Gloria's husband was a solicitor, much older than she was. In fact he was senior partner at the office where I worked. We handled Gloria's affairs. They didn't amount to much. She was a schoolteacher. Her mother died. She bought a flat. That sort of thing. No big deal. But Gerald Alexander took a fancy to her. When his wife died, Gloria moved in. He was a nasty bit of goods. Rotten as an employer, even worse as a husband. Gloria certainly earned her prosperous widowhood."

"I was very fond of Gerald," protested Gloria with a faint echo of her earlier exuberant manner, "and very grateful to him. You've never really done him justice, Jill. After all, one has to be careful with money when one is running a business of any sort, and—"

"Blah, blah, blah," interrupted Jill. "Never mind. Treasure his memory if it makes you happier. He was a mean old bastard, Paula, and we were both very relieved when he died."

"How did he die?" The words were out of Paula's mouth before she could stop them.

Jill gave her sudden harsh laugh. "Not of natural causes, you will be intrigued to hear. Though actually he did have high blood pressure and a heart condition, just like Gloria. But unlike Gloria, who doesn't fuss about it, he wanted everybody to know."

"He was frightened. It's very frightening, having angina."

Gloria sounded agitated. If this conversation continues, thought Paula, it won't do any good to Gloria's condition. Was that Jill's object, to bring about a fatal heart attack? Pre-sumably the money and the Mercedes and the house belonged to Gloria, and surely Jill would have made sure that she would inherit. If, as was now being hinted, Gloria had in some way contributed to her husband's death, with or without Jill's help, then she was totally in the younger woman's power. In fact each was in the power of the other, but Jill was much the stronger and the cleverer.

And the younger. Forty. Had her story, in which the woman of forty was in fact the victim, yet been in some way self-revealing? Forty was a landmark, a time to make one's hopes come true; and in Jill Freebody's case those hopes—

"Gerald was drowned."

It was Gloria speaking, and Paula felt that this absolved her from having to change the subject.

"He was fishing. It was his favourite amusement."

"Got him out of the house," put in Jill.

"I don't know whether you've done any walking around Winsford," went on Gloria, "but if you go upstream along the river from the back of Frances's house, you get to where it widens out between wooded banks. That stretch of water belongs to an angling club."

"More like a drinking club," put in Jill. "A gang of silly old men who spend far more time in the Shepherd's Rest telling about their fishing triumphs than they've ever spent by the water."

"Some of them are like that," agreed her friend, "but Gerald was not. He took it very seriously. He had a boat—a small punt. He used to paddle it out a few feet from the bank and anchor there. He had cushions and a thermos flask and sandwiches, and a radio and newspapers if he wanted to read."

"All home comforts." Jill overtook a slower-moving vehicle. They were on a fairly straight road, and perhaps it was not really a very risky manoeuvre for such a powerful car, but nevertheless it made Paula anxious, for she was inclined to be a nervous passenger.

How glad she would be to get back. Frances's cottage appeared in her mind as a haven. Even Frances and Andrew niggling at each other was a lesser evil than being with her present companions. She had expected to be bored and irritated, but she had not expected to be frightened. The strength and malice of Jill, the weakness—both mental and physical—of Gloria, and the overall sense of menace arising from all that they had told her, all combined to make Paula feel very apprehensive indeed.

They turned into a narrow road, and on a signpost she read, "Winsford—6." Not much longer now, but time enough for her to hear the end of the story of Gerald Alexander, which both ladies now appeared determined to tell her.

"The boat sank," said Jill. "He was sleeping, no doubt, and didn't notice the leak until it was too late. It was a bright but chilly autumn afternoon—rather like today—two years ago. Nobody else on the water. Nobody saw anything, so what really happened will never be known."

"Never be known," echoed Gloria. Her voice sounded rather slurred; was she having another attack?

That was Paula's last rational thought before the crash.

## 7

Paula was not detained in hospital. She was X-rayed and given painkillers for the headache and the bruising and allowed to go home with Andrew Coles, who turned out to be very good in an emergency.

"I've no idea where we are," she said as they came out of the door marked "Casualties" into what looked like blackest night.

"You have been in the South Wiltshire Hospital five miles southwest of Salisbury," replied Andrew, "and you are about to get into a five-year-old Vauxhall Cavalier to be conveyed to Winsford. I forget the exact distance, but it will take us about twenty minutes, since I intend to drive with the utmost care."

"Thanks," said Paula shakily. "I'm awfully sorry about all this, Andrew. What a blessing you were there!"

"Yes indeed. Even Mama had to acknowledge that, much though she dislikes the thought of me being any use at all, and particularly of me driving you. Would you like to sit back or front?"

"Front, please."

Andrew fixed the seat-belt and patted her hand. "Poor Paula. I know how it feels. I was in a smash-up myself a few weeks ago. D'you want to talk about it? Or would you rather wait and tell the police? They'll probably be turning up later on this evening."

"What's the time?"

"Half past nine."

"Is that all? It feels like tomorrow night. If you see what I mean."

"Yes, honey. You're a bit confused. I think you'd better sit quiet now and go straight to bed when we get back and I shall run up and down with hot milk and brandy."

"Tea, please," muttered Paula, "but no cream cakes."

Andrew made no comment on this somewhat puzzling remark, and Paula said no more. Whether as a result of shock, or because of the sedatives given for that shock, she dozed all the way, and was still very sleepy when they arrived at Brookside Cottage.

Frances was at the door to meet them. "Thank God you're safe!" she cried, and put an arm round Paula.

"Andrew drove beautifully," said Paula. "He's looked after me like an angel."

"I'm not talking about Andrew. Oh Paula, I shall never forgive myself."

Somewhere in Paula's confused consciousness were the questions she had to ask Frances, but all she said was, "May I go to bed, please?"

"Of course. I'll come up with you now. If the police constable turns up," she added to Andrew, "tell him that she's asleep and he'll have to come in the morning."

"Okay, Ma. You're the boss."

Paula thought that Andrew winked at her behind his mother's back, but it might simply have been that all her perceptions were now so muddled and uncertain that she could not distinguish thought from fact. That Frances barely limped at all as she came, one step behind Paula, up the narrow cottage stairs, was, however, definitely fact. Paula knew that it was a most significant fact, but she could not remember why, nor did she care.

It felt as if she had been many days away from the little attic bedroom, which seemed to have been her haven for a very long time.

"I wonder what happened to Timmy."

She did not know whether she had thought this or said it

aloud. Frances's face turned into a face in a dream, and she relived the crash again and again, against a background of a shifting mountain of cream pastries, and with the sound of harsh mocking laughter ever present.

"I've been permitted to bring your breakfast," said Andrew, "with instructions to tell you that on no account are you to move."

"Thanks," said Paula vaguely, as she struggled to remember who he was and where she was.

"Have I had concussion?" she asked, when her surroundings had come more into focus. "I do feel awfully muddled."

"You've had a bang on the head." Andrew poured her tea. "It's not at all serious, but you can make more of it if you want to."

"You mean, pretend I don't remember anything?"

"That's right. Think about it. You've got a couple of hours at least before the police arrive. Ma and I decided to wake you up in good time to give you a chance to assemble your wits."

"Buy why should I pretend not to remember, Andrew?"

Through her headache Paula was, in fact, beginning to remember very clearly.

"I think you'd better put that question to my mother," was Andrew's reply. "She's the one who is caught up in some peculiar web of intrigue and suspicion centred on the Merle House writing class, and she's feeling very guilty indeed at having dragged you into it."

"You mean she really did fake that accident to herself?"

"That's right, honey. Crazy, isn't it? If she'd wanted you to stay and help her try to find out what's going on, why didn't she tell you straight out? She knows you love mysteries. All she had to do was to wave one right under your nose. You'd have stayed to help her, wouldn't you?"

"That rather depends," said Paula, taking a slice of toast, "on what sort of mystery she had to wave. I do have a job to do, you know."

Her mental confusion had now almost entirely gone. She felt very weak, and disinclined for any physical effort, but the sense of nightmare had receded, and the events of yesterday were now quite clear in her mind.

"Do you know, Andrew," she added irrelevantly, "that

when we met in the car-park of the Shepherd's Rest yesterday afternoon I didn't think I was going to like you at all. The feeling was mutual, wasn't it?"

Andrew looked a little embarrassed. "I don't usually get on very well with my mother's friends," he said.

"Nor with your mother, but it looks as if that might be changing somewhat."

"Thanks to you, yes. Mama has openly confessed that my aimless way of life has never done anybody any harm, whereas her scheming to get you involved in the Merle House set-up might well have—"

"Well it didn't," interrupted Paula. "I'm alive and well. But what nobody has yet told me is whether everybody else is. What happened to Jill and Gloria? And to Timmy?"

"I think I can hear her coming upstairs," said Andrew. "I guess I'll leave her to tell you."

Paula could not blame him for escaping. He had done enough good work to deserve a break. She braced herself to stand up to Frances's self-reproaches, and to their changed relationship. Frances the strong, reserved teacher had turned into a worried, over-emotional woman, capable of errors of judgment, even capable of deception. That did not mean that Paula would not forgive her, and in the end, perhaps, love her all the more for her weaknesses, but it did mean that it would take a lot of getting used to.

Fortunately Frances seemed to understand this and to do her best to ease the transition.

"I must have been quite insane," she said. "My only excuse is that I was desperate to have someone around whom I could trust completely, and I could think of nobody but yourself."

"You could have trusted Andrew."

"I realise that now. But we'd got so at cross-purposes that I couldn't ask him. Would you have believed me, Paula, if I had told you straight away? Suppose you hadn't met Lady Hindon and seen the set-up for yourself. Would you have believed that she was stage-managing a sort of classic detective story denouement with a confession of murder? Would you have believed it, Paula?"

"I don't think I would have," admitted Paula. "Not then. But after yesterday I'll believe anything."

"Yesterday." Frances shuddered.

"But I wouldn't have deserted you," said Paula. "After all, I was going to come to the class in any case."

"I know, but that wouldn't have made any difference. You see, I had been given a part to play. I was supposed to—supposed to—"

Paula waited, but Frances seemed unable to continue.

"I'll tell you later," she said. "The main thing is that you are all right and that you've forgiven me."

"I shall withdraw my forgiveness," said Paula, "if you don't instantly tell me what has happened to Jill and Gloria and Timmy."

"Good Lord. Don't you know. Didn't they tell you at the hospital? Didn't Andrew?"

"No!" almost screamed Paula. "They didn't."

"Oh dear. Well, Jill's been kept in hospital. Slight concussion and a couple of cracked ribs. She'll be there for another few days. Timmy's all right. Rupert is looking after him."

"And Gloria?"

Paula gave herself the answer to this question even as she was asking it.

"Gloria is dead," said Frances. "The door burst open when the car hit that tree and apparently she hadn't fastened her seat-belt properly. She was thrown out, but they think she'd died of a heart attack before that."

"Yes, she had angina," said Paula, surprised at her own calmness. "She had a slight attack while we were having tea in Salisbury, and the last thing I remember clearly is thinking she was about to have another."

"The driver of the other car," went on Frances, "wasn't hurt at all. It was his fault, of course. He was coming round that corner much too fast and Jill swerved to avoid him. A few yards further on and you'd only have ended up in the ditch, but on that corner, if you remember, there's only the steep slope of trees going down to the river."

"I remember," said Paula.

"There've been several accidents at that spot, but the only way to widen the road is to buy some land off the couple who own the house opposite, and they won't sell. Though maybe they'll change their minds after last night. They were just coming out of their drive and were nearly involved in it too."

Paula was only half listening. An idea had come into her mind that she was going to keep entirely to herself for the time being. It was only an idea, based on yesterday afternoon's conversation with Jill and Gloria. She had no facts to back it up; there was no need to pretend not to remember, for she really did not know what had happened just before the crash.

"I'm making you tired," said Frances, picking up the breakfast tray. "You must rest now. I wish you didn't have to talk to that policeman."

"That's all right," said Paula sleepily. "I've really very little to tell him."

P.C. Grover was young and fair, slow-moving and slow-speaking. Several times Paula nearly dozed off while he wrote down everything she said in longhand.

"We had been talking about fishing, I think," she said. "Mrs. Alexander and myself mostly. She seemed quite well but soon after we turned into the Winsford road I remember thinking that her voice sounded slurred, as it had done when she had that attack in the cafe in Salisbury. And that's all I remember, except an awful pain in my head, and that feeling of being moved. I suppose they were putting me in the ambulance."

"Did you see the other car at all?"

"No," said Paula.

"At what speed were you going?"

"Oh—not very fast. About thirty, I suppose. One doesn't think about it when one isn't driving."

"Did you feel it was an appropriate speed for that stretch of road?"

"Yes. Just about right."

Battered though Paula felt, her mind was functioning quite clearly, and she had no desire to accuse Jill Freebody of careless driving. If Jill had committed an offence, it was a much more serious one than that. Very likely there would never be any proof, either that she had helped Gloria to dispose of her husband, or that she had somehow contrived that Gloria herself should die; and indeed, it was she herself who had brought up the subject of Gerald Alexander's death, thus arousing Paula's suspicions.

But that might be a clever gambler's double bluff. A more serious objection to Paula's theory was the fact that Jill could not possibly have known that a car was going to come round that corner at speed just at that moment, thus giving her every excuse to turn her own car off the road. If she had indeed been acting deliberately, and not in automatic response to the situation, then it must have been a matter of split-second decision-taking. Perhaps she might learn something from the young policeman.

He had finished writing. Would she like to read through her statement now? He assured her that he had written down exactly what she said.

"I'm sure you have," said Paula. "No, I won't bother to read it. My head aches too much. I'll just sign it if you'll tell me where."

When that operation was completed, she asked, "What does Mrs. Freebody say about the accident?"

"Just what you said—that she was driving along the lane at about thirty miles an hour when a car came from the opposite direction at a much greater speed and she tried to avoid it."

"And there was nowhere to turn to except a steep slope. What do you think one ought to do in such circumstances?"

The fair young man looked rather puzzled. "Well, I guess there's not much else you could do."

"What would you have done yourself?" persisted Paula. "I'm sure you're a very good driver—you have to be, don't you? Could you possibly have prevented the accident, or at any rate minimized its effects?"

"The best thing," replied P.C. Grover, "would have been to swing left and then immediately right so that the car tipped over the side of the road but remained at the top of the slope. With the other car going into the hedge, they'd still have collided, but there probably wouldn't have been so much injury."

"You would have done that?"

"I'd have tried to, but I might not have succeeded."

"Mrs. Freebody is a very good driver," said Paula. "I'm sure that was what she was trying to do."

"That's what she says," said the police constable. "Well, I don't think we shall need to trouble you again. Not till the inquest on Mrs. Alexander. That will probably be in about ten days' time."

"I'll probably still be here," said Paula. "I'm going to have to take a couple of weeks off from work. Will Mrs. Freebody be fit by then, do you think?"

"They seem to think so at the hospital."

Paula tried another couple of questions, but P.C. Grover was not saying any more, and after all, she thought, she was going to hear plenty about the accident from other people; in any case, the young constable had told her the one thing she most wanted, at this moment, to know.

A good driver might, with luck, have been able to avoid the worst effects.

Jill was a very good driver. Had she tried her best, but been unlucky? Or had she deliberately swung the wheel too far round to the left, thus ensuring that Gloria, already weakened from the state of her heart, and in the most vulnerable seat in the car, would not survive, but also taking a terrible risk with her own life, not to mention Paula's?

The more she thought about it, the more Paula became attached to this theory. It would suit Jill very well indeed for Gloria to die now, and in the presence of an independent witness—Paula herself.

For the rest of the day Paula slept, ate and drank, listened to the radio, tried to read and gave it up, and every now and then thought about her theory.

At eight o'clock in the evening she told Frances that she was feeling better but bored, and very much needed a change of scene.

"And some conversation," she added, as mother and son fussed around her in the living-room, making sure that she had enough cushions and that the lamp was not shining in her eyes.

"Frances," she said when they at last seemed willing to listen, "what do you know about the death of Gerald Alexander?"

"Gerald Alexander? Gloria's husband?" Frances sounded surprised. "I never met him. I've only known Gloria since she started coming to the literature class I was taking in Salisbury last winter. What about him?"

"Didn't she ever talk about him?" countered Paula.

"No, I don't think so. At least not very much. Which is rather odd when you think of it," added Frances slowly.

"You mean garrulous Gloria scarcely ever mentioned the dear departed?" put in Andrew.

"Yes," said his mother. "It is odd. When you think of all I've been told about the late Mr. Barton!"

"But there must have been some gossip when he died," suggested Paula.

"There may have been, but I'd rather a lot on my mind just then. You remember, darling." Frances turned to Andrew. "It was about two years ago. Dad had split up with that woman he was living with and gone into a clinic and they wanted me to pay the bill."

In one sentence, thought Paula, she had learnt more about Frances's life than in twenty years of placid friendship. Andrew added to the revelations.

"My father was an alcoholic," he explained to Paula. "He managed to charm a series of women into putting up with him during the last ten years of his life, after he and my mother parted finally, but they all abandoned him in the end."

"Except one," said Paula, looking at Frances, who was leaning her head on her hand and staring at the floor.

"That's right," said Andrew. "He died there. Mother paid the bill of course. She always paid. That's partly why we disagreed."

"You don't understand, darling," said Frances.

"Oh yes, Mama, I do. Only too well. But don't let's talk about it now. Paula wants to talk about Gloria's husband. Didn't he die while out fishing?"

"Yes." Frances seemed not sorry to be diverted from her own affairs. "The boat sank and he drowned. I'm afraid I can't tell you any details, Paula. I didn't even see the account in the papers. I was much too preoccupied. But Mrs. Barton would be able to tell you, I'm sure."

Andrew made a face.

"I don't want to talk about it to Mrs. Barton," said Paula hurriedly. "We'll never get rid of her. I only want to know whether there was any suspicion of foul play, as that nice young policeman would probably call it."

Neither Frances nor Andrew could give her any information, but Andrew offered to do some research in the library and the newspaper offices in Salisbury. "It will have to wait till Monday, though," he added. "They won't be open tomorrow."

"Tomorrow. Sunday." Paula suddenly leaned forward in her armchair and gave a squeal as the movement jarred her head. "I'd quite forgotten. We're supposed to be visiting Lady Hindon. Did I tell you, Frances?"

"You didn't, and we can't possibly go. There's no need for any deception. She'll know all about the accident. In fact I wonder that she hasn't yet sent Bruce round to enquire how we both are."

"She has," said Andrew, standing up and drawing the window curtain a little to one side. "He's just arrived."

"Damn," said Frances and Paula in one voice.

"Paula got rid of him last night," said Frances. "I suppose, darling, you couldn't—"

"Okay," said Andrew obligingly. "What am I supposed to do? Freeze him out? Or knock him out?"

"Talk to him while I get Paula to bed. Where's she gone?"

Paula was already at the foot of the stairs. Bruce Wiley was high on her list for investigating, but not just yet. By the time the bell rang, both she and Frances were at the top of the stairs, and they could hear Andrew's voice cheerfully babbling away.

"Come in. I'm Andrew Coles. I don't think we've met. Have you come to ask after the invalids? I've got two of them here now. It's like a cottage hospital. Have a drink. Coffee? No, it's gone cold. There's some whisky somewhere. My mother will be down soon. She's still rather tottery, but much better than she was. She insists on looking after Paula. The lame leading the even more lame."

In the doorway of the little attic bedroom, Frances and Paula looked at each other and smiled. But after Paula had collapsed onto the bed and rested her aching head against the pillows, she glanced up and saw that Frances was regarding her with great seriousness.

"I don't know how it's come about, Paula," she was saying, "but somehow I feel that it must be your doing. I feel that you have—that you have given Andy back to me."

Her voice was very low. Could it possibly be that Frances was weeping?

"We'd got out of gear with each other," she went on. "It

was my fault. But we're truly friends again, and I don't know how to thank you. I can face anything now. Anything."

She put a hand over her eyes, turned, and left the room. There was no doubt about it, Frances was streaming with tears, which was something that two days ago Paula would never have believed possible.

# 8

Sunday morning was cold and clear. Paula woke from a long and healing sleep and got up to stand at the dormer window and watch the sun rise over the hills beyond the river. The grass at the bottom of the garden was white with dew. Frances's cat, Leslie, returning from a nocturnal prowl, trotted across the lawn and walked delicately up the stone steps, pausing occasionally to look around him or to sniff at the earth in the rock garden.

It was a peaceful homely scene, and Paula's sense of menace in the garden had melted away as completely as would the dew when the sun rose higher. Poor Frances. What a strange, twisted state of mind she must have been in, to think up this plan to incapacitate herself, and to involve her friend in it too; and how strange and wonderful it was that they could now be completely open with each other.

The husband an alcoholic—yes, that explained everything. Frances's secrecy, the fears for Andrew, the estrangement from him. Presumably Frances had led the whole neighbourhood to believe, as she had led Paula to believe, that Derek Coles had died years ago; but Lady Hindon must have discovered the truth, and by threatening Frances with exposure had persuaded her to do—

To do what?

In all their talk yesterday evening, it had never been made

quite clear to Paula exactly what it was that Frances was trying to escape when she contrived that it should be Paula alone
who went to the writing class. Jill Freebody had said that
Lady Hindon, out of pure mischief, was trying to unveil
somebody's guilty secret by setting the "murder assignment";
Frances had gone further, saying that Lady Hindon was actually aiming to secure a confession.

Did Frances know who was supposed to confess? Paula
had no doubt that she would soon know all that Frances knew.
She was feeling very much better, and her headache was almost gone, and since neither of the others seemed to be stirring, Paula decided to get up and make breakfast. She had just
completed this operation and was pouring milk into a saucer
for Leslie, when Frances joined her.

"Did you sleep well?"

"Wonderfully. And you?"

"The same."

They sat down to toast and coffee, and Paula said, "What a
nice view on a sunny morning. It takes an accident to make
one realise just what a joy this is—the little things of everyday life that we take for granted."

"An accident—" began Frances in a troubled voice.

"It wasn't your fault in any way," broke in Paula warmly.
"And I wasn't the one who was meant to die. It was Gloria."

"Paula! Are you saying that Jill crashed the car on purpose? That's even more crazy than my exploits. Besides, the
other car—"

"Let me tell you my theory." Paula pushed aside her plate
and rested her arms on the kitchen table. "I wasn't going to
mention it just yet, but I've decided now to keep nothing
back. To hell with secrecy. How's this for a scenario: Gloria
gets rid of her mean old husband."

"How?"

"Makes a hole in the boat or something. Let's take that as
read. Either Jill helps her, or else Jill gets to know she's done
it. Either way, she is in Jill's power. She's got a weak heart,
and when she dies Jill gets the house, the money, the car, the
lot. And she also gets rid of Gloria's company. Has she, or has
she not, got an excellent motive for murdering Gloria?" demanded Paula.

"Yes," replied Frances, smiling. "A superfluity of motives,

I should say. But why does she choose this extraordinarily risky method, which might well have resulted in her own death as well?"

"That's why, that's why!" cried Paula excitedly. "Don't you see? It's the classic alibi. You take some of the poison yourself, then make yourself vomit. You present yourself as a victim too, and who will suspect you of the crime? And if you've got a third party present, who will be an independent witness—well, what more can you ask?"

"I suppose there might be something in it," said Frances slowly.

"Right." Paula poured out more coffee. "Would you mind putting the objections? As you used to at school when I'd written a very dogmatic essay without enough evidence to back it up."

"I did nag at you." Frances smiled reminiscently. "But it taught you to look for flaws in an argument. Well, here goes. Objection number one. Jill couldn't possibly have known that a car was going to approach at speed round a dangerous corner."

"Agreed. The accident was not planned in advance. The opportunity was seized when it arose."

"But to think so quickly—"

"She's an exceptionally quick thinker. And it might not have been quite so quick after all. Isn't it just possible that she could have seen the other car coming at speed down the hill, round the further bend in the road? You know the road well. What do you say?"

Frances thought a moment. "I think it's not impossible," she said at last. "But heavens, what a nerve it would take!"

"She's got the nerve. We'll go out and experiment later. As regards what one can see, I mean. We won't go to the lengths of repeating the crash. Next objection please."

"You will dispose of it, I'm sure, and I think this is really the only other major criticism that I have. It's about Jill's own attitude. Assuming that she was going to kill Gloria without incriminating herself at the first opportunity. Then why did she talk so much about Lady Hindon trying to uncover guilty secrets? Why, in particular, did she tell you about Gerald Alexander's death? She seems to have gone out of her way to arouse your suspicions."

"Ah, yes. The double bluff. All part of the classic detective story. You reject the obvious suspect as being too obvious, and then he turns out to have done it after all."

"Paula." Frances chided her. "We're not talking about classic detective stories and the craft of writing them. We are talking about—if your theory is correct—a very wicked and dangerous woman. I've never much liked Jill Freebody, and I can well imagine her to be both ambitious and ruthless. But this is something more."

"To return to your objection," said Paula, "I find it a stumbling block too. On the other hand, by talking to me like that she was sort of spreading the suspicion around. She wanted to get across to me the idea that somebody in the group had something to hide—this was a fact that you confirm yourself, Frances—and she wanted me to suspect everybody, herself included. If she was the guilty one, then it was clever to get her version of the story in first. And don't forget, Frances, that it wasn't aimed solely at me. It was intended to play upon Gloria's fears and her conscience and her weak heart so that she might, perhaps—yes, that's it! Jill was working up to Gloria's suicide and confession note. But the chance of a fatal accident came instead, and was too good to miss. I'm sure that's it. Isn't it?"

"You have put forward a very convincing theory," said Paula's former teacher, just as she might have said it twenty years ago. "How do you propose to get about testing it?"

"We can check the road straight away, and Andrew can get those newspaper reports tomorrow. Otherwise—well, I hadn't really thought yet."

"Would you like to try it out on Lady Hindon?"

"Frances!"

"Don't look so horrified. I didn't mean tell her what you've been telling me. Just confine your story to what you told the police, and to the actual events of Friday afternoon. She's dying to know all about it. Bruce Wiley said last night that if we feel up to it, the invitation to tea today still stands. She will send Bruce to collect us both, and will make sure that we do not overtire ourselves. Would you like to go?"

"Would you?" countered Paula.

"I might as well get it over with. And we'll be able to support each other."

"All right then. But you really must tell me exactly what it was that she wanted you to do with the class."

"We'll talk about it when Andy's gone," said Frances.

"Andy's not leaving us?"

The events of the last forty-eight hours had brought about such a change in Paula's attitude that she was as sorry now to hear of Andrew's departure as she had previously been to learn of his arrival. But it turned out that he was only going into Salisbury to see his car-dealer friend and would be back to lunch.

"D'you want me to pump him about Gloria's husband?" he asked. "Toby's lived in this neighbourhood all his life. Fifty-five years, to be exact."

Andrew paused to enjoy the surprise on his listeners' faces. "That shakes you, Mama," he went on. "You thought he was a young tearaway. No, Toby's a very respectable company director and a magistrate. He'll probably remember the Alexander case."

Frances looked very disconcerted, and to comfort her, after Andrew had gone, Paula said, "I got the impression, too, that he had got in with some shady dealers. I think Andrew has been a bit naughty, Frances, playing the bad boy to annoy you, but that's all over now, and there are no secrets between you and him."

"Not quite no secrets. This is where I want your advice. Be patient with me, Paula. When you've bottled something up for so long it's not easy to talk about it."

Paula made encouraging murmurs, and gradually the story came out. Frances had moved to Winsford to try to build up a new life for herself after she had parted from Derek Coles. Andrew had then been away at boarding-school. These were the years, thought Paula, when her own marriage was breaking up, and she and Frances had rather lost touch at that time.

"Soon after I'd come here," went on Frances, "I had a letter from Derek. His lady friend had walked out on him and he'd been drinking heavily again and was having treatment at a place not far from here. You can imagine the sort of letter. And as Andy said, it wasn't the only time. It happened again and again. I suppose it was very weak of me to keep helping him, but—"

There was a long silence, but the thoughts of the two friends were moving in harmony.

"Right," said Frances at last. "Let's get to the point. I went to visit him at that clinic and got to know a man whose wife was there as a patient. Also an alcoholic. We talked about it, naturally, as people do when they have similar problems, and we became very friendly. More than friends. Lovers. Are you shocked at me, Paula?"

"No indeed. I'm glad for you. If it brought you comfort."

"Much comfort, yes. But also guilt. To him as well. We both had very strict and moral upbringings, and we both very much disliked the need for secrecy and deception."

"But would it have mattered—" began Paula.

"Yes," said Frances firmly. "A country neighbourhood isn't like London, where you can live next door to somebody for fifteen years without knowing anything about them. Safety in numbers." She smiled faintly. "Down here we all know each other's business. Or think we do."

Paula was not entirely convinced by this familiar argument, but she very much wanted to hear more, so she said nothing.

"His wife," went on Frances, "actually got quite a lot better and came out of the clinic. It wasn't a happy marriage. It never had been, but she was very dependent on him. Very helpless. Very nervous. There was no question of his leaving her. We both knew that, although we couldn't help hoping. We could make a good marriage, Paula. We've got so much to give each other. And he would be so good for Andrew. And Andy for him. He always longed for a son and he has no children. But there's no question of it and I must not think about it. One must not—one simply must *not* put one's own happiness onto the possibility of somebody else dying. Oh, Paula!"

"If only I could say or do anything that would help—"

"Oh, my dear, you do. It helps so much to be able to talk about it. To a sympathetic ear, I mean. Damn."

The last was in response to the telephone ringing.

"Don't answer it," said Paula.

"I must. It could be Lady Hindon."

Paula made some rude remarks about Lady Hindon, but Frances merely smiled and went out into the hall.

"I've told her we're coming to tea," she said when she returned, "and that Andrew will bring us and fetch us. She'd rather it was Bruce Wiley, but for once I've managed to be firm."

"As a matter of fact," said Paula, "I feel quite capable of driving."

"So do I, but we're both supposed to be semi-invalid, so we'll have to remember to keep it up. Now where was I before that interruption?"

"You were just about to tell me the name of the man whom—"

"I wasn't, you know. You're trying to trick me into it. I'm ashamed of you, Paula Glenning."

"Sorry, ma'am."

"I'm just wondering whether it will make it easier or harder for you if you know," went on Frances.

"Doesn't that rather depend on whether you want to deny the rumour or not? For I take it that this is what Lady Hindon has been holding over you?"

"Yes. And still is holding over us."

"It'll be much easier for me to try to help you if I know," said Paula firmly. "I suppose he's a member of the writing class?"

Rapidly in her mind she was going over the possibilities. Not Bruce Wiley himself, surely. Frances would never appeal to a man like that, nor he to her. Besides, he was living at Merle House, not at home with an invalid wife. Norman Smith, the farmer? No. Quite the wrong type. Rupert Fisher, nice open-hearted Rupert Fisher. Of course. He must be the one. A minister of religion. Of course it had to be kept secret. But how lovely for Frances. If only—

"We promised never to mention it to anybody without first consulting each other," said Frances in a low voice, "but I think Ernest will forgive me when—"

"Ernest?" Paula could not keep the amazement out of her voice.

"Ernest Brooker. It was originally Bruchmann. His people escaped from Vienna during the Nazi persecution."

"Mr. Brooker." Paula's mind was turning somersaults. "But I thought he—I mean, isn't he a personal friend of Lady Hindon?"

"A very old friend, yes. They have known each other since her dancing days. He was a rising young theatre and music critic for a weekly review and she was an aging ballerina. He would have married, but she wanted the security of a rich husband. That was her second. Ernest married a member of the corps de ballet and I don't think it was ever very satisfactory for either of them. Lady Hindon continued to take a possessive interest in him, which did not help the marriage. That was the beginning of the story. I've already told you the latter part of it."

"But what I don't understand," said Paula, trying to digest all this, "is that Ernest Brooker should come to a writing class when he was a professional writer in his own particular sphere."

"Lady Hindon told him to. Although in fact it isn't entirely a waste of time. It doesn't follow that you are any good at writing stories and general articles, just because you write about opera and ballet, and he is genuinely interested."

"How on earth have you endured the classes—both of you?"

"Ernest and I are both very reserved people," said Frances rather sadly. "Very undemonstrative. Very used to controlling our feelings. That's why we mean so much to each other."

Paula could appreciate this. She was also beginning at last to make some sense of Lady Hindon's motives. A general love of mischief-making, a power complex, both these played some part in her actions, as Jill Freebody had said, but there was a much more direct personal motive involved as well. She considered Ernest Brooker to be her own property forever. She had been jealous of his wife, possibly she had even been partially responsible for the wife's excessive drinking. Certainly she was very resentful of his relationship with Frances and was determined to destroy it.

"So Lady Hindon was holding this over you both," said Paula. "She wanted to get him away from you, and was going to expose you if you didn't do what she wanted. What exactly did she want you to do at the class, Frances?"

"She wanted me to confess—in a roundabout way of course, but making it perfectly plain to Ernest—that I had hastened on my husband's death."

## —9—

"How perfectly absurd!" exclaimed Paula after a brief pause. "You didn't, did you, Frances?" she added after another short silence.

"It would have been possible. I actually thought of it."

"Thinking isn't doing. Look at Hamlet and Macbeth. How would it have been possible?"

"The drugs they give them in the clinic can be lethal if taken with other drugs. Painkillers, for example. Derek suffered from bad headaches. He often complained that they didn't do enough to relieve them and asked me to bring him something."

"But surely he wouldn't have taken anything that he knew was dangerous?"

"People who are slowly killing themselves with alcohol are impervious to such considerations," said Frances bitterly. "He'd have taken anything that brought immediate relief."

"But you must be able to prove that you didn't give him anything. What about the postmortem?"

"There wasn't one. The immediate cause of death was stated as pneumonia."

"Well then."

"That can mean anything or nothing. In Derek's case it meant nothing, except that it sounds respectable, and the doctors at the clinic preferred it that way."

75

"Frances, you are making me quite alarmed. Do you mean they issued faked death certificates?"

"Not exactly faked. Let's say, somewhat adjusted. It's much more common than is generally realised. Ask anybody who has had long experience of coroner's work."

"I must be a very credulous innocent," said Paula. "Anyway, don't let's argue about it now. What I want to know is, does Lady Hindon have any evidence that you gave your husband any painkilling tablets?"

"None whatever. Rumour doesn't need evidence. It doesn't even need some sort of recognisable foundation. It is soundless and invisible and without smell or touch. And deadly. Like radiation."

"But surely," protested Paula, "if you and Ernest Brooker really love and trust each other—"

"I don't think it would survive the sort of campaign that Lady Hindon would wage," said Frances. "And don't forget, Ernest's wife is alive. He must be super careful if he is to avoid having her be made to suffer."

"But surely she must know. Or at any rate she must suspect."

"She doesn't know. She doesn't suspect," said Frances fiercely. "If there is the slightest risk of Lady Hindon telling her, then Ernest and I will have to part."

"Oh, Frances!" It seemed to Paula that there was every possibility of Lady Hindon doing just that. "I think it's high time," she added in lighter tones, "that somebody eliminated Lady Hindon. Any hope of that?"

Frances took this question quite seriously. "I should think quite a number of people would be glad to have her out of the way, but whether anybody has a strong personal motive, I don't know."

Paula very nearly said, "Apart from you and Ernest Brooker, of course," but she restrained herself. Frances was her friend, closer now than she had ever been. Whatever fresh revelations were to come, Paula was going to trust Frances and help her as much as she could, though she feared that there was little she could do apart from sympathise. Even if Lady Hindon did not go to the lengths of telling Ernest's wife, she thought, both Frances and Ernest would suffer dreadfully from being gossiped about. They were both so vulnerable;

quiet, reserved people who kept their feelings to themselves.

How could they stand up to Lady Hindon? Apart from her physical frailty, she seemed to have no weak spots. Paula had already had the sense of a ruthlessness in her. Unlike Jill Freebody, she was not aiming for wealth and power, for these she possessed already. Her motive must lie in her insatiable egoism; a man who had once loved her must never love anybody else.

It made sense to Paula. But with what weapons could one fight her?

"Who is Lady Hindon's heir?" she asked. "Who gets Merle House when she dies?"

Frances hesitated before she replied, and Paula had the feeling that she was not being completely frank. "There are no children, and Sir Reginald was only a knight, not a baronet, so there is no title to pass on, and there don't seem to be any close relations."

"What about Bruce Wiley? Surely he will benefit."

"I don't know," replied Frances slowly. "He seems to do whatever she wants and to be perfectly happy about it. Whether that's because he hopes to inherit or whether she has got some hold over him too, I don't know."

"Perhaps he's more closely connected than we think. An illegitimate son?"

Once again, Frances gave serious consideration to Paula's half-joking suggestion.

"I have sometimes wondered," she said. "In fact Ernest and I have talked about it. He certainly is not Ernest's son, but there are other possibilities. Lady Hindon kept her marriages and her love life in separate compartments. We have no evidence whatever, but it is certainly not impossible. The age is right, the physical appearance is not unlike."

"Do other people talk about this possibility?"

"I haven't heard them, but then I am very careful what I say and what I listen to."

"Your neighbour—Mrs. Barton?" suggested Paula.

"She doesn't have anything to do with Merle House," replied Frances, "but if there were any such rumours going around I'm sure she would have mentioned them to me."

Paula agreed. "And I think Jill would have mentioned it too," she added. "But that doesn't mean we need dismiss the possibility. Does anybody know anything at all about Bruce? Has she ever deigned to explain him, so to speak?"

"Oh yes. The provenance is impeccable. Among his many interests, the late Sir Reginald dabbled in the hotel business. Exclusive little country-house hotels. Bruce used to manage one of them, and was very willing to come and manage Merle House instead when its owner suggested it."

"Has anybody checked on that story?"

"No. Why should they? It sounds likely enough."

"It's probably true," sighed Paula. "But that still doesn't mean that there's nothing else behind it."

Frances did not reply. Paula had the impression that she wanted now to be alone, so she said that she was going to stroll down the road to test how far she had recovered.

"I won't overdo it," she promised.

In fact she very soon found that she had walked enough. This was rather disappointing, but on the other hand it justified the two weeks leave that she was taking on account of the accident. As she returned to the centre of the village, she was tempted by the sight of her own car, still standing in the yard of the Shepherd's Rest.

It would be a good idea to drive a little way, just to confirm that she had got her nerve back. Only a few miles.

But she was more agitated than she realised, flooded the mini, and took some time to get started. Fortunately there was little traffic on the road, and by the time she approached the corner where Jill Freebody had swung the Mercedes leftwards into the tree-trunks, she had almost completely regained her confidence. The crushed undergrowth, the broken twigs and branches, showed her that here was the spot. They had, of course, been travelling in the opposite direction, coming towards Winsford, and she would need to drive on a little way and then turn back.

Paula did this, and approached the dangerous corner very slowly. About twenty-five yards short of the place of the crash, it was possible to gain a glimpse of the road ahead between the trees. Paula was in luck. As she glanced up she saw a red car come into view and disappear after a very few seconds. Another few seconds and it was coming round the corner towards her, slowly and carefully. It was a little Volkswagen. The driver was a young woman with a child sitting beside her, and another, younger child, safely strapped in, in the back.

Paula mentally thanked the unknown mother. That settled one point. Jill could have seen the approaching car.

What would I have done, Paula asked herself as she drove past the accident spot again and pulled into the verge when the road became wide enough, if I had caught a glimpse of that little red Volkswageen coming down the hill much too quickly?

The answer of course was that she would have tried to get off the road, swung to the left, just as Jill had done; but since the mini was a much smaller car, and she would probably have been driving even more slowly than Jill at that point, she would probably have ended up tipped into a tangle of prickly bushes, and with luck, would not have hit any of the tree-trunks at all. She might even have escaped without injury.

Probably; with luck; might have. It was all speculation.

Paula's little spurt of satisfaction soon died away. The only way of knowing what Jill had intended was to see deep into Jill's mind, which surely nobody would ever be allowed to do. She might have contrived Gloria's death; she might, with or without Gloria, have contrived Gerald Alexander's death, but at this moment Paula felt more interested in the fate of Frances and Ernest than in the possible crimes of Jill Freebody, and her main object was to try to find some link between the two.

"Could Jill have any suspicion about you and Ernest?" she asked Frances, when she had returned to Brookside Cottage and reported the result of her experiment.

Frances thought not. "We don't look the type of person to have illicit love affairs," she said. "In any case, I don't think Jill would be interested in gossip just for the sake of gossip. It would need to have some purpose behind it."

"That's what I think. All that talk in the Salisbury cafe was done with a purpose. When did you first meet her, Frances?"

"Jill? At my Salisbury class. She and Gloria came together. She wrote some rather interesting poems. I don't at all like to think of her as a possible murderer, and I think we ought to phone the hospital and find out how she is. Andy took flowers yesterday but he didn't go up to the ward."

The report on Mrs. Freebody was satisfactory. She was

comfortable and making good progress. Would they like to speak to her?

Paula signalled "No" while Frances was being connected. The subsequent conversation was short and seemed to consist largely of Jill's enquiries about Paula.

"I just can't believe that she did it on purpose," said Frances as she replaced the receiver.

"I still think it's possible," said Paula obstinately, "but there's no way of ever proving it, even if there does turn out to be something fishy about Gerald Alexander's death."

"He was certainly fishing. Don't you think you'd better get some rest now, Paula? You're not really supposed to be doing anything."

This advice was taken. Paula was indeed feeling very tired and it was a relief to lie down and shut her eyes. But she could not control her thoughts. Do I want to believe Jill is guilty, she asked herself, because she was responsible for my own unpleasant experience? To be driving a car involved in an accident which resulted in injury and death—what a horrible thing to happen to an innocent person. Yet Paula could feel no sympathy for Jill. Why was her conviction so strong? Perhaps, after all, her mind held some memory, some evidence that shock and injury had destroyed.

Paula was worrying away at this possibility, and had temporarily put Frances's problems out of her mind, when her friend came up to say that Andrew had returned and that they ought to be getting ready to go to Merle House.

"If you're quite sure you feel fit for it," she added anxiously.

"At the moment I do. If things get difficult we can always use my sore head as an excuse to get away."

On the way, Andy told them what his friend Toby had said about the inquest on Gerald Alexander.

"He remembers it well, being keen on fishing himself. Liz —that's Toby's wife—actually dug up a newspaper report. She wants to—wait for it, Mama—write stories and articles for the papers and she's a great hoarder of possible ideas although she never actually gets round to writing anything. I told her she ought to come to your classes, but not to worry, she'll never find the time."

"She'd be very welcome, Andrew. I should like to meet your friends."

"Thanks, Ma. You shall."

"But what did it say?" asked Paula, a trifle impatiently. "The press report."

"One point of interest." Andrew slowed down for the turn into the main road. "The leaking punt actually belonged to Gerald Alexander. He kept it in the club's boathouse and nobody else would dare to use it. The other boats were the property of the club and only taken out occasionally. Most of the members preferred to fish from the bank. Gerald was the only one who regularly paddled out to mid-stream."

"Was the boathouse kept locked?" asked Paula.

"That question was asked. Everybody swore that it was always locked with only the members of the angling club possessing keys, and that no unauthorised person could ever get in."

"But you don't believe that?"

"I should think that anybody who is active and prepared to get wet, would be able to get into an old boathouse if they tried hard enough."

"I'd like to have a look at it," said Paula.

Frances, who had been uneasily silent during the conversation, protested from the back seat of the car at Paula's remark, and Paula had to promise that she had no intention of trying to swim along the water-weeds near the side of the stream, but only to walk along the bank.

"What about the punt itself," she asked Andrew. "Did they recover it?"

Andrew replied that it had been dredged up and examined. It was a very battered old craft, the dark varnish chipped, the wood rotting. Gerald Alexander's widow had testified that she had frequently urged her husband to give up using the punt. She was sure it was leaking and unsafe, but he was very obstinate about it. He had made his best catches from this old boat and was convinced that it brought him luck. He had named it "The Jolly Angler," and had himself painted the name in yellow lettering at the bows.

"No sign that anybody had been tampering with it?" asked Paula.

"There was nothing mentioned in the newspaper report," was Andrew's reply.

"But what does your friend think?"

"That the only possible verdict was accidental death."

Paula would have liked to ask further questions, but they had now arrived at the gates of Merle House and from now on her thoughts must be with Frances.

Andrew slowed down to turn sharp left between the stone gateposts. At that moment Paula was looking straight ahead along the open stretch of road, with low hedges either side. In the distance, travelling in the same direction as they were, was a yellow mini. She noticed it, idly at first, because it was similar to her own; and then she began to think that she had recently seen just such a car, and remembered her first arrival at Merle House, and her meeting with Mr. Rupert Fisher.

It could well be his mini. The colour was rather unusual. And he might even be driving away from Merle House. Certainly they had not seen the car on the road in front of them, and for the last couple of miles there had been no side-turning out of which it might have come.

They stopped on the gravel space in front of the main door of Merle House. The notion that Rupert Fisher could have been here was vaguely disquieting to Paula—she did not know why—and she tried to put the thought out of her mind.

"Who looks after this place?" she asked Frances as they got out of Andrew's car. "One doesn't see anybody about, but surely Bruce doesn't do everything himself."

"They have a rota of staff from an agency, I believe," replied Frances. "Including a night attendant for Lady Hindon if she should need help. Actually I think she is capable of doing most things for herself and can even walk a little, although I've never seen her out of her chair."

She wouldn't want to be seen struggling, like any other crippled old lady, thought Paula—it would completely ruin the image.

Andrew touched the doorbell. Bruce Wiley let them in. Paula thought he looked tired, older than he had before. He seemed to have lost some of his self-assertiveness.

"I'm glad you could come," he said, addressing Frances and Paula. "Lady Hindon particularly wanted to talk to you. She's been very restless and worried. I don't think she's at all well, but she won't give in. Would you go along to the library? I'll go and tell the maid she can bring in the tea."

Frances and Paula walked slowly along the corridor, not speaking. Each could feel the mounting tension in the other as well as in herself.

"Shall I wait here in the hall?" said Andy. "I'm only here as chauffeur."

"You're invited to tea too," said Bruce. "I won't be a minute, then I'll join you."

The door of the library was closed. Paula and Frances looked at each other and smiled faintly.

"She can't eat us," whispered Paula. "Frances—dear Frances, you are *not* to be bullied into giving up your Ernest!"

"I wish I could see what else I could do," whispered Frances as she tapped on the door and then gripped the handle.

The beauty of the room struck Paula afresh. She would have loved to be alone in it, to move around at will, to look at books or sit and think; or just sit and rest her eyes on its perfect proportions, its scholarly elegance. It was a room for the greatness of the human mind—not for its malice and pettiness.

In the grate a log-fire was burning. Several armchairs were placed near it, each with a small table by the side. Lady Hindon was facing the fire, sitting in her wheelchair with her back towards them, and she did not turn round as they entered.

Paula wondered if she were asleep. Her own impression of a very formidable personality had been so augmented by what she had since heard of Lady Hindon's life and activities, that it was difficult to think of her in terms of normal human frailty. She glanced enquiringly at Frances, who responded with a slight shrug.

The two friends stood side by side just inside the door, somewhat at a loss. It seemed almost like sacrilege to approach that still figure without being summoned, to speak without having been addressed.

Paula was the first to move. She made a little detour towards the circle of armchairs round the fire so that she should approach Lady Hindon from the side, not from behind.

"Good afternoon," she said. "What a pleasure to come into this lovely room again."

There was no response. The aged Mona Lisa was sitting in exactly the same position as she had sat before, with the long, brown velvet dress covering her feet and the long fine hands folded in her lap. Within its surround of dark hair the face looked paler than ever. The head rested against the back of the chair. The eyes were open, staring straight ahead.

Paula let fall her half-raised hand and stood still, hypnotized by that face. It was as if she stared at a picture and the picture stared back at her.

"What's the matter?" murmured Frances, stopping at Paula's side. "Is she asleep?"

"I don't know. I don't think so."

With great effort Paula took a step forward and then another. Then she unzipped her shoulder-bag, took out a pocket mirror, and held it in front of Lady Hindon's slightly parted lips.

The glass remained unclouded, showing no sign of breath of life.

"I think she's dead," said Paula.

"Good God!" exclaimed Frances. And then, as Paula moved towards the door saying they must fetch Bruce at once, she added much more quietly, "Thank God. Oh, thank God."

# — 10 —

Paula was very grateful for the tea that the maid, a quiet middle-aged woman, brought to them in the drawing-room. There was no fire in the vast room, and she and Frances sat on one of the window seats near a radiator. Bruce had gone to telephone the doctor, and Andy, after remaining with them for a minute or two, had disappeared too. They could see him now from the window, walking restlessly about the grounds.

"He's longing to go," said Frances. "Can't we just slip away? There's nothing we can do here. We're only in the way."

Paula drank some tea. Her throat felt tight and her head was aching badly again. "I don't think we'd better go until the doctor arrives," she said. "We found her. We shall have to explain."

"What is there to explain?" Frances's voice was suddenly sharp. "We happened to come into the room just after she'd had the heart attack or whatever."

"We found her," repeated Paula obstinately. And then suddenly she began to laugh. "The body in the library. The classic country-house mystery."

Frances looked at her in alarm. With an effort Paula controlled her laughter. "Sorry," she said. "I didn't mean to suggest . . . I mean it can't possibly be anything but a heart

85

attack. Or something like that. But I do think we ought to stay and see the doctor."

"All right. I wonder where Bruce is. I think I'll try to find him."

Frances put down her teacup, stood up, and walked purposefully out of the room. Paula moved into an armchair and lay back and shut her eyes. It was a relief to be alone. She wished she had not made that silly remark about the body in the library, but there had been in her at that moment a rising hysteria that she had now fortunately brought under control.

Of course Frances must be relieved, immensely relieved, that Lady Hindon was dead, and why should she not say so? When only a close and trusted friend was present there was no need for concealment or hypocrisy.

Of course Frances was glad, and Paula was glad for her, and for all other innocent victims of Lady Hindon's malice.

Innocent? Innocent of what? Or guilty of what?

Suppose this was not a natural death. Frances, at least, could have played no part in it, for she had barely been outside Brookside Cottage, and most certainly not to Merle House, since Paula's arrival at Winsford three days ago. Neither could Jill Freebody have anything to do with it, for she had been in hospital since the car crash on Friday.

Bruce Wiley was the obvious suspect. He knew how Lady Hindon lived when she was not making her public appearances, and he had a far better opportunity than anybody else had to contrive an accident for her.

Bruce had shown very little emotion when he came into the library, brought there by the maid, who had arrived with the tea-trolley almost immediately after the discovery that Lady Hindon was dead. He had stood looking down at her for a moment and then said, very calmly, "This is not entirely unexpected, but I am sorry that you should have been subjected to such an embarrassment. Would you like to sit next door for a little while? Moira will bring in the tea to you."

They had thanked him. He had said that he was sure Dr. Mackeson would come as soon as he possibly could, and that was all. No expressions of shock, none of regret. Certainly none of joy and relief. From Bruce Wiley's behaviour one might have supposed that the death of Lady Hindon was no more than some trivial little inconvenience.

But surely it must affect him very deeply, if not in his emotions, then at any rate in his circumstances. Would he benefit? Or would he lose?

Irritated by her total lack of knowledge about Bruce's relationship to his employer, Paula opened her eyes, sat up, and decided to look around. Andy was no longer visible from the window. The drawing-room did not interest her. It felt cold and formal, a show room, unrevealing of the people who lived at Merle House.

What she really wanted to do was to take another look at the library. What excuse could she make if discovered? Left her gloves? Dropped her handkerchief? Oh, why worry. It would be perfectly obvious that she was lying, whatever she said.

There was nobody in the corridor. The house felt uncannily quiet. Had Frances found Bruce? Or had she linked up somewhere with Andrew? Or neither?

Paula pushed at the library door and found the answer to these questions. Frances was standing with her back to the door, bending over the writing-desk. She turned round when Paula came in and said with obvious relief, "Oh—it's you. I just wondered . . ."

She moved towards the door and they stood together just inside it.

"You wondered whether you'd left your scarf in here," murmured Paula, "and you came to look for it. I was doing just the same."

Frances glanced at her suspiciously, and then her face lightened and she managed to smile. "We'd better not be caught. Let's go."

"Yes."

But Paula hesitated, looking round the room. It seemed to be just the same as when they had come in, expecting Lady Hindon to greet them. But yet it was not quite the same. Something was not quite in the same position. The desk? No. If Frances had been looking for something there, then she had left no evidence of her search. The drawers were closed, the green blotter was undisturbed. To its left was the little pile of papers fixed by a Victorian glass paperweight, and behind the blotter was a heavy glass pen-tray. On the right was what

looked like an engagement diary; the telephone; and a pad for
messages.

Then what was different? It was something in this area of
the room, something that one would see when staring at the
unmoving figure in the wheelchair. Paula's friends sometimes
wondered—indeed, she sometimes wondered herself—how
she could at the same time be so untidy and so observant. Her
own rooms were always in a muddle and yet she could always
find what she needed. "It's not that I don't see the mess," she
would explain rather guiltily, "I do see it—all of it—but it
just doesn't worry me."

What, then, was different here?

It was one of the chairs. The big, brown leather armchair to
the right of Lady Hindon, between her and the desk. The
cushion had been moved.

Paula had walked right round this chair when she made her
detour in order to approach Lady Hindon from in front. It was
a pale orange cushion, lightening the darker upholstery. It now
lay, correctly plumped up, against the back of the chair. But
when she had walked round it earlier, the cushion had been on
the seat, crushed-looking, as if somebody had been sitting
there.

And why not? Cushions were for sitting on. If somebody
had been in the library talking to Lady Hindon, it would have
been natural to take this very chair.

Then who had removed it from the seat, and replaced it in
its usual resting place?

Not Lady Hindon, for she was dead. Not Paula herself. As
far as Paula knew, there were at the moment only five living
people on the premises: herself and Frances; Andrew; Bruce
Wiley; and the maid, Moira.

The last-named was surely the most likely. It would be
almost an automatic action for somebody with domestic re-
sponsibilities, however temporary, to straighten curtains, wipe
up spills, plump up cushions.

Of course it must be the maid, and there was nothing of the
least significance in the fact that the orange cushion had been
moved.

Frances was tugging her arm. "Come *on*, Paula. We
mustn't be found in here."

This time Paula let herself be pulled away.

When they were back in the drawing-room she said to Frances, "You didn't really go to look for Bruce, did you? You wanted to look for something on Lady Hindon's desk."

"I suppose it was silly of me," said Frances, "to think she had written a letter to Ernest's wife and was going to torment me with it."

"You didn't find anything?"

"Nothing. Not even in the drawers. Although I dared not do more than glance into them."

Paula wished she could be quite sure that Frances was speaking the truth. It was horrible to feel that she could not completely trust her friend; even worse to feel that the distrust was mutual. If only Frances had said straight out that she was going to search the desk. They could have done it together, helped each other.

Was it ever possible completely to repair a broken trust? It seemed that sympathy and understanding had little to do with trust. Paula found herself ever more deeply concerned about Frances, more and more longing for her problems to be solved and for her to find happiness. But at the same time she could not forget that Frances could be deceitful, even towards her own friend.

"Did you move a cushion?" she asked casually.

"A cushion?" Frances looked puzzled.

"Yes. I think one of them had been moved."

Paula wandered over to one of the long windows. Andrew was coming across the lawn towards them, and she opened the window bolts and let him in. "Any sign of the doctor?" she asked.

"That's his car." Andrew indicated the Land Rover that had driven up to the house. "He's with Bruce in the hall now. I saw you two through the library window. I hope you weren't tampering with the evidence or rearranging the corpse."

"Not funny," snapped his mother, and Paula added mildly that she had just wanted another look.

"One last farewell," said Andrew. "Poor old Ma. It must have given you quite a shock, finding her like that. But at least you've been spared the tea-party and we'll soon be able to go home. Presumably she had a heart attack. Or something?"

He looked questioningly at Paula.

"I hope that's it," she said. "We'll know in a minute or two. They seem to be going in there now, by the sound of it."

She had moved towards the door of the drawing room. Andrew, who seemed to be very restless, inspected the tea-trolley, found there was no tea left, suggested ringing the bell for the maid, and when neither Paula nor his mother replied, joined Paula at the door, opened it a little way, and stood there listening.

Frances, who had sat down, got up again and joined them. In silence they stood near the door of the big drawing room, more like anxious relatives awaiting the verdict on a critically ill patient than comparative strangers who'd accidentally witnessed a sudden death.

At last Bruce appeared and they all three moved away from the door, embarrassed, as if they had been caught eavesdropping, although in fact they had heard nothing of what had been happening in the library.

"I'm very sorry about all this," said Bruce, "but Dr. Mackeson would like to speak to you, Paula, if you don't mind. We shan't be long," he added to the others.

The two things that Paula noted about Dr. Mackeson were that his hair was completely white—although he looked no more than sixty—and that he was in a very bad temper, which seemed to be directed primarily towards herself.

"You found her?" he said abruptly after the briefest of greetings. "What made you think she might be dead?"

"I didn't think she might be dead. I thought she was asleep."

"Why?"

"Because she didn't move or speak. Didn't seem to hear us at all."

"How did she look?"

Paula hesitated.

"Did she look exactly as she does now?" persisted the doctor.

Reluctantly Paula followed him past the brown armchair with the orange cushion and stopped immediately in front of Lady Hindon. There was nothing at all horrifying about the still figure, but Paula had to force herself to look closely. Most deaths, she was thinking, arouse respect for humanity, pity for its frailty, remind us that we shall all pass that way.

But not Lady Hindon's. One had no sense of shared human experience. She did not even look pathetic or frail. It was difficult to realise that she would never speak again.

"Looks the same?" snapped Dr. Mackeson.

"Yes. I think so," said Paula. "She sits so upright. I suppose she's supported by the back of the chair."

But the head does seem to be leaning back rather further than if she were alive and simply reclining against the back of the chair, Paula was saying to herself. Supposing somebody had pressed it back with that cushion. But she would have struggled. Wouldn't that have left some signs? Or had the body been arranged in its present position after death, as Andrew had suggested?

"Were the eyes open?" asked Dr. Mackeson.

"Yes."

"Take a closer look."

Paula bent forward. "They look so staring. The pupils . . ."

"Yes. Dilated."

"Belladonna?" hazarded Paula, feeling as if she was being drawn into some very odd and quite unorthodox medical consultation.

"Atropine, don't you think?"

"If you say so," said Paula. "I wouldn't know anything about it. I'm not a doctor of medicine, you know. I teach English Literature."

"Oh, you do, do you?" Dr. Mackeson transferred his glare onto Bruce, who hastily explained Paula's position.

"It looks as if I have to apologise," said Dr. Mackeson to Paula with some semblance of friendliness. "I took you for Lady Hindon's witch doctor. It's all the fault of our friend here."

"You didn't give me a chance to tell you," protested Bruce. "Dr. Mackeson and I play golf together," he explained to Paula. "He's been attending Lady Hindon for the past six months, but recently she has become interested in herbal remedies and has been consulting a practitioner."

"Practitioner!" sneered Dr. Mackeson.

"I see," said Paula. "And Dr. Mackeson jumped to the conclusion that it was me?"

"Mea culpa," said Dr. Mackeson airily, "but not exclusively my fault. He only said that Dr. Glenning was here and that she had found the body, and since these charlatans have the cheek to use the title of 'doctor'—"

"Never mind," said Paula. "Now we've got that straight, can you tell me how she died? I can't help being curious, having been first on the scene."

"Oh, the old ticker just stopped," said Dr. Mackeson. "That's the usual cause, eh?"

"I suppose so," said Paula, deciding that she disliked Dr. Mackeson just as much when he was being jokey as when he was bad-tempered.

"Now of course you are going to ask me why," he went on, "being a lady with an enquiring and academic turn of mind. Well, the answer is that I can't tell you. We physicians make no claim to magic powers. I can give a guess, and it may turn out to be correct. That's all."

He stopped speaking, and looked at her in a challenging manner that seemed to be asking for her admiration, and Paula murmured, "Yes, I see," in what she hoped were appreciative tones.

"My guess," continued Dr. Mackeson, "aided by this"— and he reached down into Lady Hindon's brown leather handbag which hung from the back of her wheelchair—"is that she had gone just a little too far in her enthusiasm for the magic concoctions."

And in an aggressively dramatic manner he thrust out his closed fist and opened the fingers to reveal a little bottle lying in his palm.

He seemed to be offering it to Paula, and she wondered whether she was supposed to pick it up.

"It won't bite," said Bruce, looking rather amused by her embarrassment. "But that doesn't mean it is harmless."

Paula bent forward. She saw a little dark bottle rather like the sort used for ear-drops or eye-drops. She could see the label, which lay uppermost. It was decorated with a design of green and yellow leaves, and in the centre was something in typescript, but from where she was standing she could not read it.

"Hyoscine," said Dr. Mackeson in a satisfied manner. "One of the alkaloid poisons. Used in some of the seasick remedies. Can be lethal in overdose. Being a literary lady, you will remember it by its common name. Henbane. The stuff that King Claudius dropped into Hamlet's father's ear. 'Juice of cursed Hebanon.'"

"Why would Lady Hindon be taking this?" asked Paula, disliking Dr. Mackeson more and more but very fascinated by what he was saying.

"As a sedative, no doubt. She suffered from insomnia and palpitations, among a variety of other nervous symptoms, for which of course I prescribed the most suitable medicaments."

"She said the pills made her sleepy in the daytime and muddled her brain," said Bruce with a touch of malice, as he glanced at the doctor.

"Well at least they didn't kill her. She's only been taking the correct dose, judging by what is left."

"So what did kill her, then?" asked Bruce.

"Her fatal habit of mixing it," replied Dr. Mackeson. "We'll have to check up on this, of course, and I'll have a word with the coroner, but I don't think there's much doubt that a few drops of this home-brewed poison combined with the very suitable sedation that I prescribed have had a lethal effect."

"Will there have to be an inquest?"

"H'm." The doctor massaged his chin. Like a bad amateur actor overdoing the part, thought Paula. "We may get away without one," he went on. "I know the coroner well. But don't you worry, my dear."

He turned to Paula and put on a patronising manner. "Even if you are called to give evidence, there's nothing in it. Nothing at all. You just say exactly what you've said to me and you'll be all right. Nothing to worry about at all."

Paula bit back a sarcastic retort. She was dying to know how Lady Hindon had obtained the little glass bottle, but felt that it would be wise not to ask anything outright.

"If you don't need me anymore," she said to Bruce, "then Frances and I will be getting home. Goodbye, Dr. Mackeson."

Bruce apologised again as he accompanied Paula out of the room. "It seems very unfair that you should have been subjected to this ordeal," he said. "Particularly so soon after your accident. You'll begin to wish you'd never come to stay in Wiltshire. And I'm sorry about Jack Mackeson. Can't think how that misunderstanding arose. He's not a bad sort, really. At least he's managed to last out for six months. Lady Hindon goes through doctors like some women get through husbands, and we were running very short of applicants for the job when Jack Mackeson came to practise in the area."

They paused in the corridor, outside the library door.

"He doesn't like alternative medicine," said Paula.

"That's putting it mildly! But then most doctors are the same. Personally I think there's a lot to be said for the less orthodox forms of treatment. Acupuncture, for example. It did wonders for a cook we used to have here. Completely banished her migraine."

He pushed at the drawing-room door, nearly colliding with Frances and her son, who were still standing there.

Further apologies were uttered, and when at last they were on their way home Paula told them about her encounter with Dr. Mackeson, and Bruce's remarks about Lady Hindon and doctors.

Frances in particular listened with great attention.

"I think I can guess where she got the hyoscine," she said when Paula had finished.

"You can?" exclaimed Paula sharply.

"I said I can guess. Of course I can't be sure. Melanie King is often at Merle House, and she's recently become very interested in herbal remedies."

# 11

The telephone was ringing when they got back to Brookside Cottage. Frances picked it up and made a face at the others while she listened. Then she said, "All right then. Come round in about ten minutes' time."

She turned to Paula and Andrew. "Well, well. News of Lady Hindon's death has already reached Winsford, it seems. That was Mrs. Barton next door. She's just had a phone call from Terry asking if she wants him to come and do some gardening tomorrow, and incidentally informing her that he was over at Merle House this afternoon because his mother was doing a temporary domestic job there."

"The maid," said Paula.

"Presumably. That's village life for you. Everybody is always connected with everybody else."

"If Mrs. B. is coming in to chat," said Andrew, "then I'm going out. Sorry, Mama, but I can't take it."

"Neither can I," said Paula. "I'm going upstairs to rest."

"You are all deserting me," said Frances reproachfully, but she did not look at all unhappy.

In fact, she looked as if she had got what she wanted. She looked serene, almost glowing—much more like the old confident Frances Coles whom Paula had known years ago. Of course she was rejoicing in Lady Hindon's death. She was only waiting for Andrew to return to his car and Paula to her

95

bedroom so that she could telephone Ernest and tell him the news before Mrs. Barton arrived.

And Mrs. Barton? What was she to be told? The story about Melanie King and the herbal remedies, said Paula to herself. Frances was going to make sure that everybody knew. Why else should she be so willing to talk to the gossiping neighbour just at this moment?

"I'm going upstairs," said Paula again. "See you later."

She hated the way her thoughts were moving; she would have liked to talk to Frances completely openly about Lady Hindon's death, as openly as they had discussed Frances's love for Ernest. On the drive back from Merle House she had believed this was what they were going to do—to talk at peace and at leisure. But Frances didn't want this. She had chosen to talk to the neighbour instead, knowing very well that both Andrew and Paula would keep out of the way.

Paula shut her bedroom door behind her. The headache had come on again quite badly and she felt rather ill. She swallowed two of the painkilling tablets that she had been given at the hospital, and lay down on the bed. For a couple of hours she slept on and off, vaguely conscious now and then of the telephone ringing and of movement in the house. When she came down she found a peaceful domestic scene. Frances was sitting reading, with the cat on her lap, and Andrew was sitting on the floor, fixing a new plug to the flex of the television.

They greeted her kindly, hoped her headache was better, wanted to make almost as much fuss of her as they had done the previous day. Nevertheless Paula had the sense of being the odd one out, as if they had been discussing her in her absence and were somehow in conspiracy against her. For her own good, of course, and with the best possible motives.

Andrew's next remark bore out this suspicion.

"Mama and I have been talking, ever since she got rid of Mrs. Barton," he said, putting the finishing touches to his task. "We've decided that this part of Wiltshire is not the best place for a peaceful convalescence at the moment. You could have done without this afternoon."

Paula had to admit that it had been a great strain.

"Ma is feeling it too," went on Andrew. "The phone rings nonstop and it's going to get worse rather than better. What you both need is a few days to recover while I stay here and deal with enquiries. Mama knows a small hotel in Bournemouth which is quite tolerable. She didn't want to suggest it herself because it might look as if she was trying to turn you out. So I'm suggesting it for her."

Andrew pushed in the new plug, switched on the television for a moment to check that it was in order, and then got up and sat on the arm of Paula's chair.

"Nobody is trying to make you do anything you don't want to," he said, smiling at her. "It's only a suggestion."

"It's quite a good suggestion," said Paula cautiously, while her thoughts raced ahead. He'd doing this very well. Nice boy. Even if my friendship with Frances doesn't survive, I'm glad I have met Andrew. And that I know he will keep an eye on her. But what do I say now? How to keep calm, to appear friendly, but not to fall into the trap.

Frances wanted her out of the way. Now that Lady Hindon was dead, her whole life and expectations had changed, and she wanted a simple straightforward reason for the death; or if that was impossible, then she wanted any gossip to be about somebody else—Melanie King, for example—and not about herself. She did not want Paula nosing around. This was quite understandable. Even in less dramatic circumstances, friendships had to give way to serious love affairs. True friends understood this very well and supported each other. But true friends did not exploit and hurt each other, as Paula was feeling hurt and exploited now.

But it was her own fault. She had set Frances on a pedestal: a superb teacher and an inspiration to the hopeful but timid scholar that Paula herself had once been.

The young Paula had loved and admired and been enormously grateful. She had known nothing of the older woman's human frailties. And in her relationship with Frances, it was the young Paula who had survived all these years and never wanted to grow into an equal.

But it was not just the young Paula who was feeling so keenly now the pain of being made use of and then rejected. This lack of trust was right here, now, in their relationship as equal adults. It had been overshadowing them both, a dark cloud, ever since Paula's arrival. Once or twice it had dispersed and the light of true friendship had broken through, but now it was there again, darker than ever.

Paula looked across at her friend.

Frances had not even raised her head while Andrew was speaking. Her book now lay on the side table and she was stroking the cat, cradling the head in one hand and passing the other hand again and again along the thick, bright orange fur.

The orange fur—the orange cushion.

Paula's mind went back to Lady Hindon's library and she instantly pushed the thought aside. If it was not the drugs that killed Lady Hindon, but somebody making use of the weakened state induced by the mixture of drugs, then that somebody could not possibly be Frances, because Paula herself had been with Frances during the vital period of time.

Could it be Ernest?

The moment this thought came into Paula's mind she knew that there could be no bridging of the gulf that had arisen between Frances and herself, and this meant that she knew how to respond to Andrew's suggestion.

"I could certainly do with a few days without any fresh shocks," she said, "but I don't particularly want to go to Bournemouth. I think much the most sensible thing is for me to go home, and then perhaps I can come and stay here for a night or two when they hold the inquest on Gloria Alexander. And if there has to be an inquest on Lady Hindon too—but I'm not going to worry about that now. One thing at a time."

Andrew gave her a grateful glance. It seemed that she had said just what he wanted her to. But Frances began to protest that this wasn't the idea at all; she didn't want to lose Paula's company, it was just that they needed a break, both of them, and they were clearly not going to get much peace in Winsford at present.

"Then why don't you go to Bournemouth yourself?" suggested Paula, trying hard not to allow the slightest trace of resentment to appear in her voice. "Truly I'd much rather go home. I shan't be going back to work just yet, but it'll be a treat to have all my books around me and plenty of time to read."

Frances continued to protest. The insincerity was obvious and Paula began to feel quite ashamed for her and grateful when Andrew intervened.

"Paula wants to go home, Mama. And she knows you don't really want to go to Bournemouth either. What's worrying me is whether you are fit to drive, Paula. Would you like me to run you up to London tomorrow? I could drive your mini and then come back here by train."

"That's very kind, Andy," said Paula, meaning to thank him not only for the offer, but for his making it look as if she was going of her own volition and not because Frances wanted her to. "I'd rather drive myself, though," she added. "I'll take it very slowly and make lots of stops."

At this moment the prospect of a couple of hours driving on her own was very attractive to Paula. It would be a great relief to be right away from human relationships and human passions. As far as Lady Hindon's death was concerned, Paula could only hope that Dr. Mackeson was correct in his assumption that it had been caused by an injudicious mixing of drugs. The other recent death, that of Gloria Alexander, would be dealt with at the inquest that Paula would be obliged to attend. There was no need to stay with Frances or with anybody else. She could get an early train to Salisbury and go home when the hearing was over.

She was just about to say this aloud to Andrew when the telephone rang yet again. Frances got up to answer it, leaving an indignant cat lashing his tail on the floor. As soon as she was out of hearing, Andrew whispered to Paula, "I don't think Mama really meant to drive you away. But she's in a very peculiar mood."

"It's all right, Andy. I want to go. Honestly. Your mother and I are better apart just now. I'm a horribly inquisitive creature and I think she feels I know too much."

"If you say so, honey. Personally I'm very sorry you're going. Of course she doesn't want to go to Bournemouth. But I can't make out if she wants me to stay here or not. What do you think, Paula?"

"I don't know, Andy. Perhaps she'd rather be alone. Why don't you ask her?"

They had no time for more. Frances returned and said that it was Jill Freebody telephoning from the hospital. She had heard the news of Lady Hindon's death, of course, and was longing to hear more about it, but quite apart from that, she particularly wanted to talk to Paula. Did Paula feel up to it?

"I can hardly pretend I'm not well enough for a telephone conversation," replied Paula, "after I've been gadding about the country finding corpses."

In fact she was grateful for the distraction. At least she had no close personal involvement with Jill Freebody. There were no long years of gratitude to remember; there were no recent startling revelations; there were no hurt feelings.

She sat down on the chair in the hall and picked up the receiver.

"Hello, Jill. How are you feeling?"

"Much better, thanks. They're letting me out tomorrow, provided I have somebody living in to look after me. Gloria's daily woman is going to come and sleep in. She's rather a fusspot, but at the moment I don't think I shall mind that. But what about you, Paula? Are you feeling better?"

Paula gave a guarded account of her own condition since the accident, and added that she was going back to London tomorrow.

"Oh. I'm so sorry." Jill sounded disappointed. "I'd hoped to see you. I very much wanted to apologise."

"Whatever for?"

"Well, first of all for driving you into a concussion."

"But it was an accident. You couldn't help it."

"It was an accident. That's true. It really was an accident. But I still feel—"

She broke off, and Paula, feeling rather bewildered, could think of nothing to say.

"I can't talk on the phone," went on Jill. "There's all sorts of people milling around me here and I've no doubt that you are being overheard as well. I suppose there's no possible chance of your looking in on me before you go?"

"This evening? Isn't it rather late for visiting?"

"It would be all right this end. But how would you get here?"

"I could drive, I suppose," said Paula very doubtfully. In fact she was longing to go to bed. A warm drink and solitude and sleep. That was all she felt fit for. The thought of a hospital visit involving fresh revelations and prolonged apologies was more than she could bear.

"No, of course you can't come here tonight," said Jill in her abrupt manner. "You're still only convalescent. Tomorrow morning? It's on your way to London. If you could bear to stop off for a little while I'd be very grateful indeed."

"All right then. About eleven o'clock?"

"That would be fine. I just want to explain something. I promise not to let you in for any big dramas. Goodnight. Many thanks, and sleep well."

Paula replaced the receiver. How quickly do circumstances and feelings change, she said to herself. If anybody had suggested even a few hours ago that she could ever feel quite warmly towards Jill Freebody, she would have said that was impossible. Yet now she was viewing the morning's visit, if not with enthusiasm, at any rate with goodwill. She was also curious to know what Jill was going to say, and for this too she was grateful.

Curiosity was a great reviver. Her depression began to lift a little.

"I'm going to call in on Jill in hospital on my way home tomorrow," she said as she came into the kitchen, where Frances and Andrew were laying out a cold supper.

"That's very kind of you," said Frances.

"D'you think she's going to make a confession to you?" said Andrew.

"She seems to want to apologise for my getting concussed," said Paula.

"Quite right, too." Andy opened a can of beer with a flourish. "If she wanted to get rid of Gloria she ought to have had the decency not to let anybody else get hurt."

"Maybe she didn't want to get rid of Gloria. It's only our theory."

"I'm sure she's going to make a confession."

"I sincerely hope not. Very exhausting, listening to confessions."

They continued to talk about Jill and Gloria and the late Gerald Alexander throughout the meal, in the same half-joking, half-serious manner. Thanks to Jill's phone call, this last evening at Brookside Cottage was much more tolerable than it might have been. Lady Hindon's death was not mentioned. Paula had the feeling that Andrew wanted to talk to her alone, but she gave him no chance. When Frances took the telephone extension into the sitting-room and shut the door behind her, Paula said she must go up and pack and then to bed. If there were to be problems again between Frances and her son then they must sort them out for themselves.

The little attic bedroom was cosy and welcoming. Tomorrow night, thought Paula as she looked into drawers and cupboards to check that she had left nothing behind, I'll be able to relax at home and forget that I ever met the members of the Merle House writing class.

But of course she could not forget. The moment she shut her eyes the images came. The beautiful elegant room. The wide eyes of the dead woman. The orange cushion. Frances standing by the library desk. Frances rejoicing. Dr. Mackeson's dead white hair. The plain, placid face of the middle-aged maid who turned out to be the gardening boy's mother. The little dark bottle. And Frances saying it came from Melanie.

And a car driving away from Merle House. A mini like her own. Rupert Fisher's. What sort of car did Ernest Brooker drive? Perhaps he and Rupert were friends and had been there together. And one of them had sat on the chair next to Lady Hindon. The chair with the orange cushion. Orange. Frances sat there too, with her hands moving slowly over the soft orange fur.

The images became more and more confused. The reasoning faded completely, and Paula drifted into an uneasy sleep from which she awoke at dawn, feeling cold and deeply depressed.

She washed and dressed quickly and went downstairs to make tea. Neither of the others was stirring. The sight of the garden with its steps reminded her of her arrival. What a horrible, miserable visit. She wished with all her heart that she had never come.

Suddenly she could not bear the thought of seeing either Frances or Andrew. She tore a sheet off the telephone message pad and hastily wrote down the first words that came into her head.

"Woke early feeling much better—decided to get moving at once. Will phone you this evening. Love, Paula."

She left the note on the kitchen table, picked up her suitcase and her handbag, and silently let herself out of the house.

# 12

The only sign of life in Winsford on this misty Monday morning was the milk delivery van. Paula collected her mini from the yard at the Shepherd's Rest and watched the milkman carry a little crate of milk bottles across to the door of the inn. This struck her as incongruous until she recollected that a lot of their trade nowadays consisted of coffee and lunches, and presumably the manager's family would use milk for cooking and for breakfast cereals.

What a pity they were not open for breakfast. Paula thought longingly of a large bowl of cornflakes with brown sugar and creamy fresh milk. The only place where she could be sure of finding food at this hour, however, was a motorway service station.

She looked at her watch, consulted the map, and planned what to do until it was time to visit Jill. The best hope for breakfast seemed to lie on the main road to Salisbury, the way they had taken when they went to the tea shop. It would mean doubling back a little to go to the hospital, but with three hours to kill, and feeling physically much better than she had since the accident, Paula decided that this was no great hardship. She folded up the map, drove out of the car-park before the milk van could block the narrow lane, and came up the steep hill into the main road. After a couple of miles she found

103

what she was seeking, filled up the tank of the car, and drove round to the back of the cafe.

The first vacant space she saw was alongside a car very similar to her own, a mustard-coloured mini of an older vintage but looking now as if it had been washed. Inside the cafe, at a table near to the entrance, sat the Reverend Rupert Fisher, staring rather disconsolately at the menu.

"Do you mind if I join you?" asked Paula.

He looked startled at first, then beamed.

"What a pleasure! I was just wishing I'd stayed at home for breakfast, but your arrival changes all that. This place is not what it was. They've no longer got kippers. What are you going to have?"

"Cornflakes, eggs and bacon. The whole lot. I'm ravenous."

"I'll join you." He gave the order to the girl in the bright red overall who came up to the table, and then said, "What brings you out at this hour?"

"I'm going home to London and wanted to start out early, but didn't want to disturb the household."

"And I'm doing the same, except that I haven't any household to disturb. I look after myself and I was just too lazy to make my own breakfast. What a pity we can't travel together and share the cost of petrol. It seems silly to make a procession of yellow minis along the London Road."

Paula explained that she was not going straight on, but had a call to make first.

"Ah. Pity. Then we shall have to part. I have to be at a meeting at noon. A gathering of the clans from all over Europe. And some from further afield, I hope. It's an organization concerned with religious freedom. And every other kind of freedom too. We get together every so often to make public pronouncements and forge private friendships. The latter are much the more important. You know the sort of thing."

"It's just the same with teachers' conferences," said Paula as their breakfast arrived.

"You've not had a very happy visit to Wiltshire," said Rupert presently. "In fact it's been just one series of disasters, though I hope you didn't regard coming to our seminar as one of them."

"No indeed. That was a pleasure."

"But you could have done without the car crash and the ordeal at Merle House yesterday afternoon." He put down his coffee cup and looked at her with sympathy. "I know all about it, you see. Probably more than most people. Mrs. Carson, who is a neighbour of mine, helps at Merle House at weekends, and as she hasn't got her own transport and it's an awkward cross-country journey, I drive her there whenever I can."

"So it was your car that I saw disappearing when we arrived at Merle House," exclaimed Paula.

"Very likely. What time was that?"

"About half past three. Perhaps a little later."

"We were rather on the late side. I had been taking a service for a colleague of mine who was unwell, and kept Mrs. Carson waiting. She was worried, because Lady Hindon doesn't like unpunctuality, but I knew Bruce would smooth it over for her. He's a good fellow. Very diplomatic. Needs to be, in his position."

"You didn't go into the house yourself?"

"Lord, no. I never do. Only for the writing class. I'm not in the proper social category to visit on equal terms, and I certainly wouldn't accept an invitation on any other."

"Our invitation did seem rather like a royal command," said Paula. "I gather from Frances that most invitations to Merle House are like that."

"All invitations," corrected Rupert. "She has no living relatives and no real friends. Poor woman. I doubt if she has ever been capable of friendship, as you or I know it. Even her husband—but I don't want to bore you."

Paula assured him that she was very far from being bored, and Rupert assured her that he had time for a fresh supply of coffee, and when this had been ordered, he continued.

"Lady Hindon was a very lonely woman, one of the loneliest I have ever met, and I've come across many in my pastoral work over the years. I think she suffered from the very worst kind of loneliness—lack of anything to love. Perhaps lack of the capacity of loving anything. People tend to think that loneliness comes from losing those you love, which of course it does, or from not having anybody to love you, which of course it does again. These bring terrible pain. But it is—somehow—a living pain, not a dead emptiness. The dead emptiness comes from deep within, when there is nothing and nobody that truly touches the heart. That's the end of my sermon. Thank you for your patience, Paula."

"Do you think we all of us, now and then, suffer from this very worst form of loneliness?"

"Many of us, at any rate. Fortunately it is usually only temporary."

"Then I think I know what you mean. I have fits of depression sometimes, and it feels just like that."

"I do too, when the picture of my dear wife looks nothing but a blank to me. But you wanted to hear about Merle House. You've seen for yourself what sort of a feudal setup it is. We all of us played our parts, not stepping outside our serf-like roles. Your good friend Frances included. I think we even quite enjoyed our play-acting in a way. We certainly enjoyed the classes. But I don't think there was anybody—except perhaps Ernest Brooker—whom Lady Hindon regarded as anything approaching an equal to herself."

"Ernest Brooker? Frances told me," went on Paula, anxious not to appear too deeply interested, "that he is a drama critic and essayist. It's not my field, but I am rather surprised that I don't know the name at all."

"No, you wouldn't. He uses another name to write under. It's not my field either. But I believe he stands high in his profession. I expect you also know that Lady Hindon used to be a ballet dancer, which may account for her rating English more highly than we lesser mortals."

Particularly if they were once lovers, thought Paula, but she did not say this aloud, for she had the impression that Rupert had not the slightest suspicion of this.

"What about the others?" she asked. "Wouldn't Mrs. Alexander, for instance, be regarded as something like a social equal? Her husband seems to have been acceptable in the best circles."

"Nouveau riche, dear Paula. And Gloria herself came from quite the wrong background. A mere teacher. Like you and Frances."

"Melanie King, then."

"Ah. A borderline case. Only a nurse, of course, but her mother was distantly related to one of our local aristocratic families. Probably the nearest to a female friend that Lady Hindon has had in recent years."

"And your own friend Norman Smith is obviously out. Who is left? Oh, of course. Jill Freebody."

"Way beyond the pale. A jumped-up typist. But extremely intelligent. And with some of the qualities of Lady Hindon herself. I think she recognised a worthy adversary there. Poor Jill. I hope she is feeling better. That is surely every driver's nightmare—to be, however innocently and indirectly, the cause of another person's injury or death."

Paula agreed, and promised to convey Rupert's good wishes to Jill before continuing with her inquisition.

"How about Bruce? What sort of man is he? I find him rather puzzling."

"Bruce is a hangover from the days of Sir Reginald, and he was inflicted on Lady Hindon rather against her will. He used to be Sir Reginald's right-hand man in his hotel enterprise. He is extremely competent, but he had some sort of breakdown, and since Sir Reginald felt rather guilty about this, and liked him personally, he offered him the job at Merle House. I think Lady Hindon would have liked to get rid of Bruce after Sir Reginald died, but she knew she would never find a replacement, and somebody had to look after the place." Rupert chuckled. "You should hear Moira Carson talking about the way the staff are treated."

"Really? I had the feeling that although she was a tyrant, she was a benevolent one. All right as long as you served her well."

"Not a bit of it. Tyrant is right, but she was dreadfully mean. Made any excuse not to pay their wages. That's why they have this rota of part-timers. No permanent staff would ever stay."

Paula remembered her encounter with Dr. Mackeson, and Bruce's remark that he had lasted for longer than most other doctors. "If Lady Hindon was so good at sending people away," she said, "it's a wonder that the writing class survived."

"It wouldn't have gone on for much longer. It was working up for some sort of crisis. Engineered by Lady Hindon because she was beginning to get bored with it. Good heavens —it's half past nine. I'll have to go. Perhaps you'd join me for lunch one day when you come down to Winsford again?"

Paula thanked him and promised to get in touch. As they

stood at the counter waiting to pay their bills, she asked, "What did Mrs. Carson say about Lady Hindon dying suddenly? Was she very surprised?"

"Very surprised. If she hadn't been late in arriving, she would have gone straight to the library, and it would have been she, and not you, who found her. But as it was, Bruce was waiting for Moira at the back door, and told her she was to start making the sandwiches for tea immediately. She says he actually stayed to help her. You people were expected any minute, and there seems to have been a bit of a panic in the kitchen."

Paula would have liked to ask more. She was very curious to know, for instance, whether Bruce went anywhere near the library during the time the maid was preparing tea, but to do this would be to show an unjustified curiosity, and in any case, Rupert would almost certainly not know the answer.

Besides, she was going home to London. She was not going to interest herself any more in Lady Hindon's death.

The girl came to take their money. Paula said goodbye, and drove away from the cafe feeling comforted. It was good to hear a view of Lady Hindon that was charitable, yet realistic. Rupert's remarks had enabled Paula to see the events of the last days in a different light, with Frances and her affairs forming only a part of the picture and not necessarily the most important part.

Lady Hindon had been a woman with no friends and very many enemies. Some of them might have even stronger reasons than Frances and Ernest to wish for her death. And if anybody really had contrived to bring it about, that person must surely be her nearest, though not her dearest. In short, Bruce Wiley.

Unless perhaps Melanie . . .

Paula herself had noticed a certain degree of gentleness in Lady Hindon's attitude towards Melanie King, and Rupert was probably right in saying that she was the nearest that Lady Hindon had to a woman friend.

A nurse. Interested in herbal remedies. Suppose that Lady Hindon knew that in a few months or even weeks she was going to die in great pain. To whom would she turn? Not one of the doctors with whom she had quarrelled, but to a woman for whom she had some tender feelings and who had—so it was rumoured—come to the help of a sister in a similar situation.

Paula turned the car into a lay-by in order to sit and think at leisure. The more she thought about this theory, the more it appealed to her. If one took Rupert's view of Lady Hindon as a bitterly lonely and unhappy old woman, not simply a malicious tyrant, then it made sense to imagine her wishing to end her life.

But what about Melanie? It was inconceivable that she should once again mercifully assist somebody to die. Unless Lady Hindon had threatened or bullied her into it, which seemed not impossible. Poor Melanie. If it did turn out that she had provided that little bottle, she would receive no mercy from Dr. Mackeson or from anybody else. All those who wanted Lady Hindon out of the way would see her as the perfect scapegoat.

Paula lit a cigarette and watched the traffic go by, the small cars passing her with a swish of air and a slight vibration, the big trucks shaking the whole roadway.

Supposing, she said to herself, that I had been in the position of Frances or Ernest; or Bruce, or Melanie, or maybe even Rupert himself, or anybody else who might have reason to wish Lady Hindon dead. One of the rejected doctors or ill-treated domestic staff, for example. How would I contrive her death without putting myself into the position of being accused of it?

Her mind went back to the stories produced by members of the writing class. Plenty of ideas for an "accidental" domestic murder there, but none of them fitted this particular case. Melanie's came nearest. I wish I knew more about her, said Paula to herself. And then: I wish I knew more about Bruce too. And Rupert, who is so nice and friendly, and very understanding, but supposing he too has been in some way a victim of Lady Hindon? He says he left Moira Carson at the back door of Merle House and then drove away, but that may not be true. Perhaps he went round to the front. Perhaps Lady Hindon herself let him in, through the library window. She could move about by herself if she wanted to.

No. That was no good. If she had taken too many sedatives, she would have been too sleepy.

Suppose she had left the window open for him, not realising that the drugs would so soon take effect. In he would come, nobody seeing him. Bruce and Moira Carson were very busy in the kitchen, and there was no one else on the premises.

He is expecting to find her wide awake. This meeting has been agreed on. It was to be a confrontation, concerning a— a . . . Well, never mind for the moment. Assume she has got some hold over Rupert and has been tormenting him. But he finds her very sleepy, not at all fit for talk. Perhaps she has had some sort of heart attack. Perhaps she is dying. She has nothing to live for; she is making so many other lives miserable.

Perhaps she is already unconscious. He comes closer, just as Paula herself did a little while later. But she is breathing. He thinks how little it would take to bring that shallow, uneven breathing to an end. He sees the orange cushion in the chair next to her. He picks it up and holds it over her face. There is no struggle. After a while he checks that the breathing has ceased, the heart stopped beating.

And then he must hurry. The risks he has taken, the enormity of what he has done—all this floods back into his mind. He drops the cushion back in its chair. He is not a very observant man; he notices people's feelings, not their outward appearances. He does not see that the cushion is crumpled, nor does he see that Lady Hindon's head is leaning back in what would surely be an uncomfortable position if she were alive.

He lets himself out of the library window and shuts it behind him and drives away. He has been, perhaps, ten minutes in the house. He is very lucky not to have been seen.

It is all perfectly possible but I just don't believe it, said Paula to herself, throwing away her cigarette. In the first place, the library window would have remained unlocked if that was what had happened.

But perhaps it had indeed remained unlocked. She had been nowhere near the window when she found Lady Hindon dead. Neither had Frances. Nor had she gone near the window when she came into the library later and found Frances there. Had Frances been near the window? Paula did not know.

Frances and Rupert in league together?

Nonsense. This is just getting silly, Paula told herself severely, and in any case you are going back to London and have got to stop thinking about what has been happening at Merle House.

She started the car. The thought of returning to London did not attract her at all. Why on earth had she become so stupidly emotional over Frances yesterday? Why had she allowed this estrangement to develop? She ought to have agreed to Andy's suggestion about going to Bournemouth. Or, even better, she should have said straight away, "Frances, you're trying to get rid of me. You're afraid I'm going to do one of my snooping jobs and find out something you don't want me to. Listen, you've been confiding in me. I'm happy that you have. You know you can trust me. Don't stop trusting me now."

If she'd said something like that instead of rushing away with hurt feelings, they would have sorted it out between them, and been all the closer for it.

It wasn't too late to say something like that to Frances now. It would be more difficult than it would have been last night, but she was going to try to do it. After her visit to the hospital. It would mean a lot more driving, but it would be worth it. Anything was better than to part from Frances in this miserable state of misunderstanding.

# ─── *13* ───

Jill Freebody was up and dressed and sitting in a chair beside her bed at the far end of the ward. She looked as neat and self-contained as ever, but when she got up to greet Paula, it was obvious that she was moving with difficulty.

"Yes, it is painful," she said in response to Paula's enquiries. "But it's nothing like as bad as it was. I'll be able to manage with the help of Mrs. Flanagan. Shall we go along to the day-room? There's never anyone there and it's much more peaceful than it is in the ward."

Paula agreed, and they made a slow progress along the corridor.

"Have you had many visitors?" Paula asked when they reached the little sitting-room, which was indeed unoccupied but smelt smoky and stuffy.

"Not many," replied Jill, collapsing into a chair. "You're allowed to smoke in here." She opened her handbag and offered Paula a cigarette. "It's good of you to come," she went on. "How do you feel about driving? Has the accident made you very nervous?"

"It did at first. But I'm back to normal now. I'm sure you'll be all right once you get started."

"That's the usual theory, isn't it? If you fall off a horse you've got to get on again at once or you'll never ride again. I'll start driving as soon as I can move freely. But I think I'll get a small car. It was Gloria who enjoyed swanning around in limousines. I'd be happy with a mini. How do you find yours?"

Paula replied that it suited her fine, and Jill remarked that she and Paula were much the same height and that it was a nuisance not to be taller. A trolley with a coffee urn was being wheeled past the open door, and Paula got up and procured two cups. So far, this meeting was turning out to be quite undemanding. Jill on her own, she decided, was much more agreeable than Jill as Gloria's companion, though she doubted whether the reverse would have been true. Gloria alone would have been hard going. But they really must talk about Gloria now; surely that was what she had been summoned for.

As if she had been reading Paula's thoughts, Jill said, "I'm going to miss Gloria. She irritated me beyond all reason but I'd got used to teasing her. I'm not a nice character. I need somebody to tease. So did Lady H. But she went too far with it. Do you think somebody killed her, Paula?"

"I don't know," replied Paula abruptly. "I suppose it's possible."

Why prevaricate, she added to herself—there's no need to do so with Jill. With all her faults, at least she's no hypocrite, and it will be a relief to talk freely.

"I hoped you'd say that." Jill crushed out her cigarette. "I'll have to hurry—we won't be left in peace much longer. I'm very glad you're all right. It was rotten for you to get dragged into this and I felt very sick about you being hurt. As for Gloria—well, that's my worry, not yours. I daresay my conscience will stop kicking at me one day. Of course I didn't crash the car deliberately, and of course she could have had a fatal heart attack at any moment in any case, but all the same..."

Jill lit another cigarette before she went on. "It's rough justice, in a way. I'm quite sure that Gloria helped Gerald to drown. She knew all about that leaking boat. She had a key to the boathouse. She was no fool, you know, behind all that chatter, but a very determined and practical person. She wanted Gerald's money and then she wanted to be rid of Gerald. And she wanted to be rid of me too, but I stuck."

Jill paused again. "It suited me to live with her. I like comfort and security too, and I hadn't had much of it up till then. Don't be afraid, Paula. I'm not going to tell you my own sob-story. Anyway, that's all in the past, and now that Lady Hindon is dead, Bruce and I can get married."

"You and Bruce!"

"Yes. Didn't you suspect? I thought you might have guessed."

"Absolutely not. Why on earth should I link you up with Bruce Wiley?"

"I don't know, I'm sure. I suppose one is so conscious of one's own little intrigues that one can't believe other people don't notice. Lady Hindon was the great obstacle, of course. Hence the secrecy. Not that she ever had any love for Bruce. In fact she hated him most heartily. But he was indispensable to her. She wouldn't have lasted a week without him. Not since Sir Reginald died. Bruce never wanted to get stuck in such a position, but it happened."

"Did he hate her?" asked Paula.

Jill gave her short, rather unkind laugh. "Did he poison her, do you mean? He says he didn't. I hope that's true."

"He's been to see you?"

"Three times since the accident. The first two times he was in a great state of nerves in case word should get round to her that he had come here. But yesterday evening, after I'd spoken to you . . ."

Jill smiled. "Oh, that was good. To feel free. I rather care for Bruce, you know. And I mean to look after him," she added fiercely. "He needs looking after. People think he's very self-confident and even rather brash, but he isn't like that at all. It's a shell to cover up his sense of inadequacy. Sir Reginald understood that."

Paula, after taking a minute or two to adjust to Jill's revelation, was thinking of things she wanted to ask, but it was too late. An old woman, helped by a nurse, was coming into the room, and when she had sat down, she first wanted to talk, and then wanted to watch television, and Jill said that in any case she had better get back to the ward.

When they reached it, Paula asked how she was getting home. "Mrs. Flanagan is going to take me in a taxi," Jill replied. "She's coming at two. Bruce would have fetched me, but he's tied up all day with Lady Hindon's solicitors. He'll be coming over this evening to report."

"Is your engagement to remain a secret?"

"Yes, please. For the time being."

Jill sat down on the edge of the bed and shut her eyes. Paula thought she looked very exhausted, and glanced around for a nurse. The ward sister was coming towards them. She looked at Paula suspiciously and then leant over Jill and touched her arm.

"Mrs. Freebody—I'm afraid we've rather bad news for you. Mrs. Flanagan has just telephoned to say that her daughter has been taken ill and has asked her to look after the children, so she won't be able to come and stay with you tonight. Do you know anybody else who could come?"

"Not unless I get someone from a nursing agency," replied Jill slowly. "But I think I could manage on my own."

"You can't possibly manage alone," said the ward sister firmly. "If you can't make any other arrangements, we'll have to keep you in for another few days. Fortunately we don't need the bed."

Paula could sense Jill's desperation. She would have been feeling just the same in that position, aching to be out of hospital and back in her own life.

"Does Mrs. Freebody need any nursing?" she found herself asking the ward sister.

"Well, no. But she's not fit to be alone."

"Then would it help if I were to stay with her for a day or two until other arrangements can be made?"

Paula spoke half to Jill, half to the sister, and saw surprise and disbelief on both faces.

"I was planning to go back to London today," she went on, "but I don't really feel up to it and would rather wait a little longer. I was in the accident too," she explained to the sister, "and your Casualty Department looked after me."

Jill, recovering herself, continued with the explanation. "And I'm going to accept Dr. Glenning's kind offer," she concluded. "May we go home at once, please? I'm all packed and ready."

The ward sister looked as if she would like to make an objection to this suggestion, but could not think of any. Jill was given various instructions and cautions, reminded that she had an appointment in the Outpatients Department for the following Monday, and finally allowed to depart, with Paula carrying her bags.

When they got to the main door of the hospital Jill paused in her slow and painful progress, took a deep breath, and said, "Ah—freedom!" before she moved on down the steps. Before getting into the mini she paused again and looked at Paula.

"I don't know why you are doing this and I think you are quite crazy, but thanks all the same. Thanks, Paula. Thanks."

Paula laughed. "I don't know why either. The impulse suddenly came over me."

In the car Jill said, "You don't really have to stay, you know. It was only to get me out of the clutches of that dragon of a sister. I can manage on my own until tonight. Then I'll get a nurse in. Bruce will fix it with the agency he uses for Lady Hindon."

"Would you prefer that?" asked Paula as they drove away from the hospital. "I don't mind staying with you at all. In fact I'd rather like to. I'm very intrigued with the Merle House situation and am longing to ask you more about it. But if you'd rather be rid of me and my curiosity, of course I shall understand."

Jill did not immediately reply, and they continued for several miles in a silence that Paula found quite restful. It's strange, she was saying to herself, that the seemingly unsympathetic characters can sometimes be the easiest ones to be with. So many people, behind a veneer of unselfishness, were in fact very demanding, and the unselfishness was aimed at making you feel guilty. But Paula felt sure that Jill, who did not pretend to any virtues, would only ask for help when she really needed it and would accept it without fuss.

Of course she was a schemer. What her motive was in telling Paula about her engagement to Bruce was not yet clear, but she had certainly not schemed to get Paula to take her home. That had come as a complete surprise to them both. And Paula also felt sure that her feeling for Bruce Wiley was genuine. It fitted in with Jill's nature. No passionate attachment, as she believed Frances's love for Ernest to be, but a sort of fierce maternal protectiveness, denied other outlets, that had fixed itself upon Bruce and his need of her.

What was she thinking now?

They had to stop at a traffic light. Paula glanced sideways

at Jill and saw that her eyes were closed and she looked very white.

"Sorry," she muttered as they moved on. "I'm a bit sick. Hope I can last out."

Paula said no more. They came through Winsford, passed Brookside Cottage, and she noticed that Andy's car was no longer standing outside. On the outskirts of the village she slowed down and said,

"I'm sorry, Jill, but I've got to ask you the way. I've never been to your house."

"Yes." Jill roused herself. "About half a mile and then turn sharp left. There's a Shell service station opposite."

Paula found the turning. It was a steep road up out of the valley in which Winsford was situated.

"Those white gate-posts," said Jill. "On the right."

Paula drove between them. To the left-hand post was secured a small brass plate with the words "River View" engraved on it. The house was built into the hillside, a long low one-story house of light Cotswold stone, with a steeply sloping roof. A new house, very conventional.

"Excuse me," muttered Jill as Paula stopped in the drive.

She stumbled out of the car, made her way, swaying a little, to the door, let herself in, and reappeared a minute later looking better.

"Just made it," she called out to Paula, who had parked the mini outside the garage and was now taking out the bags. "Many thanks. Come on in."

River View had been built and lived in with money and professional advice, but not with love. It was strange how one could tell. Frances's cottage, thought Paula, was lived in lovingly. And even at Merle House—in the library, at any rate— one had the sense that somebody really cared for the room.

Lady Hindon must have loved that room, even if she loved nothing else. She had responded with genuine warmth to others' praise of it. But had she herself chosen to die there?

So ran Paula's thoughts as Jill pushed open one door after another.

"Dining-room," said Jill, opening a light oak door upon a showpiece from a furniture store, right down to the requisite arrangement of beech leaves and chrysanthemums standing on the sideboard.

"Sitting-room."

Paula glanced across an expanse of mushroom-coloured carpet and through a wide picture window at what was presumably the river view. It consisted of a slope of gold and brown trees and bushes, with the merest glimpse of some muddy-looking water. There were no books in the room, she noticed; only some glossy magazines lying on a coffee table.

"Gerald's study."

Here were the books, plenty of them, together with a large leather-topped desk, a line of fishing-rods hanging on the wall, some sporting prints, and a stuffed salmon in a glass case. It was rather like a stage-set for the room of a retired solicitor turned angler, but at least it didn't look so clinically characterless as the other rooms that Paula had been shown.

"Your bedroom," said Jill.

"Thanks," said Paula, feeling it was high time that she made some remark. "Then you want me to stay?"

"Yes, please. At any rate, for tonight."

"It looks very comfortable," said Paula, surveying the light carpet and the frilled divan cover and the white and gold closet fittings.

"Oh, yes. Every comfort. As they say in the ads for the old people's homes. Don't bother to be polite. It's a ghastly house, isn't it? Gloria's choice. Gerald thought she had such good taste that he actually let her spend money on it."

Paula was rather glad to hear the spitefulness in these remarks. It showed that Jill must be feeling better. "Is there anything I can do for you?" she asked.

"I'd love some real coffee after that dishwater in the hospital. I can make it if you'll do the reaching up to the cupboards. My chest feels armour-plated in all this plaster, and it hurts like hell to raise my arm."

She led the way back to the door at the left of the main entrance. Paula followed her into the kitchen, and could see at once that here was the heart of the house, the focus of its life and interest. The general impression was of lemon-yellow and cream, light but not stark. Even the kitchen machinery—the fridge, the freezer, the microwave, the food-mixers and the cream-makers and all the rest of the apparatus—did not have quite such a hard laboratory look as usual.

A cookery-book lay open on one of the dresser-tops; near

to it were some sticks of parsley in an old marmalade jar, and a much-scored wooden chopping board on which lay an equally ancient bone-handled knife.

Jill glanced at the recipe-book. "Oh, yes," she said. "I was going to make a prawn omelette that day. I knew we'd have been stuffing so many cream cakes in Salisbury that we wouldn't want much supper. How very strange. It seems like another life. Accidents do bring time to a stop, don't they?"

Paula agreed, adding to herself: So Jill did the cooking, and this kitchen was her domain, not Gloria's.

"The coffee's up there," went on Jill, pointing to one of the cupboard doors, "and if you could get me down the grinder . . . thanks a lot. I can manage now."

"Did you design this kitchen?" asked Paula.

"More or less. Gloria wasn't interested and Gerald let me do what I liked provided it didn't cost him anything. I paid for most of the equipment myself, and then forged receipts for him to see—about one-tenth of the real price. He never guessed!"

Jill laughed as she said this. It was not her usual brusque and rather cruel laugh, but a little outburst of genuine amusement.

"I like cooking, and I'd got the money from the sale of my flat. There are some cups just behind you, by the way."

Paula found them.

"And if you would carry the tray—"

Paula did so.

"Lovely coffee," she said, when they were settled in the sitting-room.

"It's one of the few things that Gerald wasn't mean about," said Jill. "This was his favourite brand and we've stuck to it ever since. I say 'we' but of course it's only 'me' now. How odd it feels. I don't really believe that Gloria is dead. I've known her almost all my life. We were at the same school. I was a very raw junior and she was a very mature sixth-former. I was in awe of her then. But that all changed over the years."

Jill spoke jerkily, pausing a moment after each short sentence, not looking at Paula, and seeming to be scarcely aware of her presence.

Could she talk like this, wondered Paula, if she had planned Gloria's death? Or even if she had merely hoped for it? It seemed very unlikely. This was no false sentimental effusion concealing guilt. It rang very true. And by her own admission, Jill had loved to tease Gloria. Was it not very possible that Gloria liked to irritate Jill? A sort of love-hate relationship. Often these were the sort that endured the longest.

"I hate living on my own," said Jill, sounding even more angry than upset. "I'm going to miss her a lot."

"But it won't be for very long. You won't miss her when you move in with Bruce."

"Move in with Bruce! Me live at Merle House? You must be joking."

"Not entirely. If Lady Hindon left the estate to him, and if you're going to marry him—"

"I'm certainly going to marry him, and it's equally certain that she hasn't left him the estate. He'll be lucky if he gets this month's wages."

"But if she hasn't left anything to Bruce, then who is going to inherit?"

"Big question. That's what I hope Bruce is discovering this very moment. If not, then I'll have to phone somebody in the office myself. I'm still friends with the partners' secretaries."

"The office? Oh, you mean Lady Hindon's solicitors are Gerald Alexander's firm, where you used to work?"

"Of course. The best lawyers in the neighbourhood. Nothing but the best for our Elsie."

"Elsie?" said Paula, and then hurriedly went on, telling herself to stop echoing Jill in this stupid way. "It doesn't sound like the right name for Lady Hindon at all. She ought to have been Antoinette. Or Sonia. Or even Olga. Something vaguely exotic and slightly sinister."

Jill laughed. "She wasn't, you know. She really was Elsie. I typed one of her earlier wills, before Gerald retired. That was some years ago. I believe she'd made a lot more since then."

Paula put down her coffee cup. "Jill, you are teasing me," she said reproachfully. "You know that I am incorrigibly inquisitive, and you are holding out the most tantalising gobbets of information and making me jump for them like—like a performing dolphin. It's not fair. I've done you a good turn. I don't deserve this."

"No, you don't. I'm sorry. Gloria was so easily baited that

I've got into the habit of indulging my nastier instincts. Okay, Paula, so you want to hear what I know about Lady Hindon's affairs. Pour me another cup of coffee and I'll tell you."

Paula was suddenly struck with compunction. "Oughtn't you to go and rest?"

"I'm resting. It's not sleep I need now. It's a bit of life and interest. Stop fussing, Paula, and listen."

## — 14 —

"Sir Reginald used a law firm in London, of course," said Jill, "but after he died Lady Hindon wanted to have somebody local whom she could summon to Merle House whenever she felt like it, and she asked their advice. They suggested Gerald Alexander in Salisbury. She sent Bruce to the office to have a look at him, and that's when Bruce and I first met—in Gerald's waiting room. I didn't take to him at all. He was putting on a sort of big boss act, very much despising this small-town law business."

"Where are the offices?" Paula wanted to know.

"Just off the Market Place. Bernard Smith—that's Norman's brother—is Senior Partner now. He will have drafted all the last wills and testaments since Gerald retired. Bruce was to meet him at midday. Half an hour ago."

"Norman Smith's brother—so that's another link-up with the writing class," remarked Paula.

"Well, obviously. When Lady H. got Frances to write around asking people if they'd like to join a class to be held at Merle House, she gave Frances the names of people she thought might be interested."

"But I thought you said you and Gloria had been to Frances's class in Salisbury."

"Yes, we had. That's why we were interested. We knew that Frances was a good teacher."

"Then was it you who suggested that Frances should take the class?"

"No, of course not. I wasn't on calling terms with Lady Hindon. Bruce suggested her, and between them they thought up a list of people who might like to come. Some of them joined and some of them didn't."

"So the class was Lady Hindon's idea?"

"Entirely. She thought it would provide her some amusement. And so it did. Honestly, Paula," she went on, as Paula continued to look doubtful, "there's nothing sinister or mysterious about the getting together of the writing class. Lady Hindon was always looking for something to pass the time— amateur dramatics, sketching parties in the grounds, even a string quartet—anything that would tempt people to come to Merle House so that she could get to know them and interfere in their private lives."

Paula thought this over. It sounded very plausible indeed. In fact, it tied in very much with what Frances had said, but Frances had not told her—perhaps she had not known—in quite such detail the origins of the class.

"What about Rupert?" she asked Jill.

"Friend of Norman's. They play chess together. They lost their wives about the same time."

"And the two people who didn't come last week—I can't remember their names."

"They came through Melanie. And don't ask me how Lady H. and Melanie first got together, because I don't know and neither does Bruce. They've known each other for years. Ditto Ernest Brooker. You know he's quite an author in his own right, and this group of stumbling amateurs was hardly his scene, but Lady Hindon pulled him in and I must say he took it very well, and entered into the spirit of the thing, so to speak. But your poor friend Frances didn't like it one little bit, and I don't blame her. It's not much fun being in company with your secret love right under the eyes of a jealous harpy. It was much easier for me and Bruce. We were much less vulnerable."

Paula said nothing. She had been so sure that Frances's secret really was a secret from everybody except Lady Hindon and herself, that Jill's remarks had come as an unpleasant surprise. Poor Frances. Paula's heart went out to her friend, and she began to wonder what was going on at Brookside Cottage now, and to wish she was down there in Frances's crowded little sitting-room, instead of sitting in this showpiece of a house talking to a woman she did not really like.

And did not really trust. Just because I appreciate Jill's directness of manner, said Paula to herself, and find her easy to get on with because I can be equally straightforward with her, this does not mean that I need believe everything she says. Forget about Gerald Alexander's death. One could speculate forever and come no nearer to the truth. Forget, for the time being, about Gloria's. If Jill had intended it, then nobody was ever going to be able to prove it. Paula had seen for herself the type of quarrel-relationship that there had been between the two women. For all she knew or had noticed, Gloria might, in those last seconds before the crash, have grabbed the wheel herself and swung it round too far. If any new facts were to come out, then they would be produced at the inquest.

Jill was not interested, at this moment, in proving to Paula her essential innocence in the case of these two deaths. It was the death of Lady Hindon that was uppermost in her mind, and as Jill talked, Paula had the feeling that she was irritated because she had not got the full measure of Lady Hindon; there was something she did not understand about her.

Was it just irritation? Was there not also an element of fear? After all, if somebody had hastened on Lady Hindon's death, then the obvious suspect must be Bruce. Jill must know this only too well, and must know that Paula knew. It must surely be her chief motive, now, to divert any possible suspicion away from Bruce and onto other people. That was why she was talking so openly now, getting her story, or rather, Bruce's story, in first. It might well be a true story, but it would be angled. And in the course of telling Paula, she would find out how much Paula herself knew.

Paula had been first on the scene after Lady Hindon's death; it was important that Paula should think and act along the right lines.

Presumably all this was to have been accomplished during the visit to the hospital, not an easy task for Jill, but fate had played into her hands by removing Mrs. Flanagan.

She couldn't have known, though, that I would offer to

bring her home, argued the part of Paula's mind that wanted to think well of Jill.

No, said the suspicious part, but if you hadn't offered, she would have suggested it herself, and it would have been very difficult for you to refuse.

The silence had lasted for several minutes. Jill was leaning back in her chair with her eyes closed.

But she wasn't asleep. She was waiting to see how Paula was going to react to the mention of her friend. How should she react? What would be least damaging for Frances?

"From what I have heard," said Paula at last, "many members of the writing class felt that Lady Hindon knew more about them than they would have liked. In fact, you told me so yourself when we were having tea in Salisbury."

"Did I?" Jill opened her eyes. "So I did. Actually I was getting at Gloria. I wasn't thinking of Frances and Ernest just then."

"Did Lady Hindon know that Gloria had killed her husband?"

Jill looked surprised and not too pleased at this question. I've spoken out of turn, thought Paula—this isn't on the agenda, we are supposed to be talking about Frances and Ernest. But I won't play. I will not discuss Frances with Jill. If it comes to the point, I shall just have to say so outright. And if it creates an intolerable situation between us, then I shall just go away. After all, I'm free to go, which Jill isn't at the moment. She can't drive in her condition; she would have to rely on somebody else to take her.

"I don't know what Lady Hindon knew or thought she knew," Jill was saying. "I certainly never told her my theory about Gloria. I was never on those sort of terms with her. And I doubt if anybody else did. Not in the writing class, at any rate. I suppose she might have heard some gossip from one of the agency nurses who came in at night. Or through one of the temporary maids."

Paula had to concede that this was quite possible.

"I was going to tell you about Lady Hindon's business affairs," said Jill, "but we seem to have got diverted."

Back to square one, thought Paula; we will keep on the right track this time, but I will not say one word about Frances.

"Bruce reported favourably on Gerald Alexander," continued Jill, "and Gerald was summoned to the presence. Very delighted at acquiring such a rich and prestigious client. He found Lady Hindon a perfectly charming woman. Oh, he was quite disgusting about her. He came into my office every five minutes when I was typing that first will to hurry me up and make sure I was producing a document worthy of her ladyship's signature. The will was very long and very boring. There were lots of little legacies in gratitude to various people who had served her from time to time. A lot of charitable bequests. The bulk of the money was to go to medical research. She had some obscure sort of muscular disease which developed later in life as the result of an accident when she was young, and the people working on this were to benefit."

"What about Merle House?"

"It was to be turned into a rural arts centre. She was going through her patron-of-music phase at that time. Gerald was in rhapsodies over it. Wonderful woman. Public benefactor. Paula, I'm hungry. Aren't you? Shall we have some bread and cheese? There's a loaf in the fridge. And we'd better get something out of the freezer for dinner. Bruce will probably want a meal."

Paula was quite hungry too, and not sorry for a break in their tête-á-tête. It was much easier to be with Jill when she was moving about doing things than when she was sitting still; and in the kitchen, her own domain, one felt the good and creative side of her, and not her scheming and cruelty.

They ate together at the kitchen table, talking about Paula's job and about Jill's ambition to publish some of her short stories, and Paula gave her what advice she could.

"I'll listen to the radio stories, then," said Jill, "and have a look at some of the trade papers. And follow up the cooking ideas. Many thanks. It's been useful talking to you, but I think I ought to go and lie down soon. I'll just finish the Lady Hindon story, though. It won't take long."

"You'd got up to the first will she made with Gerald Alexander," Paula reminded her.

The break had done Paula good. Now that she was seeing Jill's motives more clearly, she felt able to frame some plan of action for herself.

"Right," said Jill. "It didn't last long. I didn't type the next will, but the girl who did told me about it. It was very different. The little legacies were the same, but the arts centre idea was out and the medical research was cut by half. The chief beneficiary was Ernest Brooker."

Paula had been half-expecting this. "Was this before the writing class was mooted?" she asked calmly.

"Oh, yes. At least two years before. Ernest and Lady H. had known each other many years. I expect you know all about that."

Jill raised her head and smiled at Paula across the kitchen table.

"I believe I do," said Paula. "He was a music and theatre critic, wasn't he? And she was in a ballet company."

"You've got it. A sort of grand passion. On both sides. I'm sure there's no need for me to go into detail. You'll have heard it all from some other quarter. And if you are wondering where I heard it from, Paula, the answer is that I am not going to tell you. But I am going to tell you why I think she altered her will so drastically at that point. It was because she had found out about the liaison between Ernest, who she still regarded as her own property—although he'd been married for years—and a certain woman who shall be nameless because you are reluctant to mention her name. Which I can quite understand," added Jill in her most forthright manner.

So we are coming to the crux of the matter, said Paula to herself; here comes the build-up of the theory—or maybe more than just a theory—that Ernest Brooker and Frances Coles were hoping that Lady Hindon would die.

"I don't quite understand," she said aloud. "How did her leaving a fortune to Mr. Brooker enable her to control his affairs? He had a mind of his own. And presumably he wasn't short of money."

"Ah—but he was. His poor wife had seen to that. Those clinics are very expensive. And Ernest earned more respect than money in his profession. He has never been a rich man."

"I've only met him the once," said Paula, "so I've no right to judge, but I do find it very difficult to see Mr. Brooker as the sort of person who would be bribed or bullied by promises or threats."

"Every man has his price. Who said that? Was it Oscar Wilde?"

"You're thinking of Wilde's definition of a cynic in *Lady Windermere's Fan*," said Paula, in the manner she might use when talking to a student. "'A man who knows the price of everything and the value of nothing.' I think it was Robert Walpole, that old cynic of a Prime Minister, who said that everybody could be bought at a price."

"Yes, ma'am," said Jill with mock humility. "I don't pretend to scholarship. I'm only a jumped-up typist."

"Sorry," said Paula, annoyed with herself and feeling that she had been put at a disadvantage. "That's the worst of being a teacher. One never really shakes it off."

"Don't I know it. You should have heard Gloria when she got going. She knew it all. But really she was rather stupid. Let's get back to Ernest. Of course he knew about Lady Hindon's legacy, and about all the subsequent wills she made, alternately disinheriting him and reinstating him. That gave her a lot of pleasure. And he had to put up with it because of his own sins. She'd got him firmly on the hook by threatening to tell his wife. And she'd have done it too."

A pause. I am not going to mention Frances, said Paula to herself; I am going to hear Jill out to the end and then I am going to leave this house.

"To which side had the pendulum swung when she died, that's the sixty-four-thousand-dollar question," said Jill. "Bruce will find out from Bernard Smith and will let me know later. The one thing we do know for sure is that Ernest had been to see Lady Hindon yesterday afternoon, because Bruce let him in. Bruce hadn't expected to see Ernest. He was expecting nobody except yourself and Frances. And Moira Carson, of course, who was to do the meals for the rest of the day. So Ernest's arrival was a surprise, particularly as it was during Lady Hindon's after-lunch rest hour, and nobody would ever dare disturb her in the library then."

Again a pause, and again Paula remained silent.

"However, Ernest said that he had had a royal summons," went on Jill, "and Bruce let him in, warning him that Lady Hindon had been taking tranquillisers recently in the early afternoons, and might well be asleep. Ernest repeated that she had sent for him. Bruce said he looked very agitated and more dried-up and tight-lipped than ever, and what any woman could see in him—but, however, there's no accounting for

tastes and he's certainly extremely cultured and scholarly and
to some people that's a great attraction. Anyway, he insisted
on going into the library. Bruce didn't go with him and didn't
announce him, and he never saw him leave so he doesn't
know how long Ernest was there.

"As a matter of fact, Bruce rather values Lady Hindon's
after-lunch rest hour, because it's one of the few times when
he can be sure of not being sent for, so that's when he
switches on one of the programmes he's videoed so that he
can watch it in peace. Yesterday afternoon it was cricket. It
bores me to tears, but Bruce is a great fan, and he wasn't
pleased at Ernest interrupting him. Particularly as he knew he
was going to have to get up again to let Moira Carson in. But
luckily Rupert was rather late in bringing her, so Bruce did see
to the end of the game."

Paula had been listening intently all the time Jill was
speaking. It was a well-planned recital. The gist of it could be
expressed in one sentence: If anybody killed Lady Hindon,
then Ernest Brooker had a very strong motive and an excellent
opportunity.

But the visit itself must surely have taken place, thought
Paula, because it would be too easy to disprove if Jill was not
telling the truth.

"Perhaps Mr. Brooker found Lady Hindon asleep and decided not to disturb her," she said aloud.

"Perhaps," said Jill smugly.

"Of course we don't yet know what killed her," continued
Paula. "Dr. Mackeson seemed to think it was a mixture of his
tranquillisers and this herbal mixture she had got hold of. I
suppose the postmortem will tell."

"Bruce said it would be today. I expect Jack Mackeson will
let him know the result. Well, that's enough for now. I'm
going to lie down for a while."

Jill looked very tired now, dragging herself up from her
chair, clinging to the edge of the table.

"Do you need any help?" asked Paula.

"No thanks. I can manage. Damn—there's the phone.
Would you mind answering it and explaining?"

Jill moved away as quickly as she could. As Paula came
into the sitting-room she had the totally irrational hope that the
call might be for her and that it might be Frances. Telling

herself that Frances could not possibly know where she was did not stifle the hope.

"Mrs. Freebody is resting," she said into the receiver. "Can I take a message? I'm a friend of hers, staying here for today."

"It's Paula Glenning, isn't it?" said a man's voice. "Jill said you'd be visiting her in hospital. Did you bring her home? That's very kind of you."

"Bruce. But she wasn't expecting you to call till this evening. Where are you?"

"In Salisbury. If you could just tell Jill—"

"No need," said Jill's voice on the line. "I'm here—on the extension in my room. Hullo there, Bruce. Do listen to us, Paula, if you want to. I've been listening to you."

The mockery in her voice seemed to be exaggerated by the telephone.

"No thanks," said Paula abruptly. "You'll be all right now."

She put down the receiver, thought for a moment, and then went into the bedroom that had been allotted to her, picked up her coat and suitcase and came out of the house. As she switched on the engine of the mini she glanced at her watch. Half past one. This was the second time in five hours that she had driven away impulsively and with a great urge to escape from where she was supposed to be staying.

But I am not going to make a habit of it, she assured herself. To Brookside Cottage now, and whatever Frances says or does, I am going to stay there, or at least within easy reach, until she is through the worst of her troubles.

# 15

The old blue Vauxhall that Andrew Coles was using took up all of the narrow parking space outside Brookside Cottage. Paula was very glad to see it. Andy would be an invaluable ally in healing the breach between Frances and herself, which was the first essential if she were to be of any use to Frances. She left the mini in the yard of the Shepherd's Rest, and reached the low wooden gate of the cottage just as the next-door neighbour was approaching her own.

"I thought you'd gone back to London," said Mrs. Barton.

"I was going," replied Paula, "but I've had trouble with the car."

"Don't you belong to the AA?"

Whenever I tell a lie of convenience, thought Paula, it always seems to involve me in further tiresome explanations.

"Yes, but it's always such a long wait for the breakdown-man," she said, "and as I did manage to get it going eventually, I though it wiser to avoid a long drive."

"You won't find Frances in," said Mrs. Barton, who hadn't been listening at all and was only wanting to speak. "She's gone off somewhere with that friend of hers who sometimes comes in the evenings. You know. Or maybe you don't know," she added with a touch of malice.

Paula could think of nothing to say, and she stood in uncomfortable silence while Mrs. Barton rummaged in her handbag for her key. Before she had found it, Andrew came to Paula's rescue.

"Saw you from the window," he said, "but as usual I was on the phone. I've left it off the hook so that we can have some peace. Come in and tell me everything. Tea? Sherry? Coffee? Whisky?"

"No thanks. Just to sit down."

"You do look rather pale and interesting," said Andy when Paula was settled in Frances's favourite chair. "I thought it was rather a daft idea, driving back to London today. Convalescence is a serious business, you know. It ought not to include finding corpses and having emotional upheavals and whatever else you have been up to since I saw you last night. Which I suspect is quite a lot, isn't it? Don't worry. Take your time."

"I've found out all sorts of things," said Paula, "but first of all, how is your mother?"

"Terrible. I've never known her like this. All caution has been flung to the winds. She asked Ernest to come over here and they've gone off together to the lawyer. He was trying to calm her down when they left, but without much success."

"Is she happy-agitated or frightened-agitated?" asked Paula.

"Both at once. She's over the moon to have Lady Hindon dead and she's scared stiff that Ernest might be suspected of having a hand in it."

"So am I," said Paula very soberly. "Listen, Andrew."

And she told him as quickly as she could, and without holding anything back at all, exactly what she had seen and heard for herself at Merle House, what Rupert had told her, and what she had learned from Jill.

He listened in silence and when she had finished he said, "Excuse me," and got up and went into the hall.

"I've replaced the phone," he said when he came back. "If anybody calls with the result of the postmortem, we shall want to know. Did you say Dr. Mackeson was doing it himself?"

"I had the impression that he would be in charge. I'm afraid I don't know the medical etiquette in these matters."

"Neither do I. But from what you say, it sounds to me as if he'd be only too happy to establish death by natural causes."

"I'm not so sure," said Paula thoughtfully. "I don't think he would want anybody to be accused of murder, but I'm sure he would like to make trouble for whoever gave Lady Hindon the herbal mixture."

"But nobody would suggest that it came from Ernest?"

"Oh no. Ernest is safe on that count. In any case, I doubt if Dr. Mackeson would go so far as suggesting that somebody was deliberately trying to poison her. Jill would be working away on that theory if she thought there was any future in it. But she isn't. She and Bruce are trying to pin a murder on Ernest. What I'd like to know is whether they suspect, or believe, that she was smothered. Do they know about that cushion?"

"You never mentioned it?"

Paula shook her head. "Only to your mother, very casually. And it seemed to mean nothing to her. In any case, Andy, there is no way that your mother could be responsible for Lady Hindon's death. Truly."

"Maybe not. But there is a way in which I could be."

"Oh, Andy, please! Don't make fun of this."

"I'm not joking. Do you remember, after Bruce let us in, that I stayed out in the garden while he put you on your way to the library? It would have been just possible, physically, for me to run across to the library window, open it, hold a cushion over Lady Hindon's face until she stopped breathing, and then get back into the grounds before you came into the library. Owing to the position of the corridor, the library window is nearer to the front door from the outside of the house than the library door is to the hall. And I don't suppose you and Mama were exactly hurrying."

Paula stared at him. "This is ridiculous," she said at last. "In any case, the window was bolted. You couldn't have got in."

"It wasn't bolted. I actually tried it. I left the front door ajar and stepped across the courtyard to the library window. In spite of what Bruce had said, I felt I was only there on sufferance and I didn't really want to join the tea-party. I tried the window because it didn't look quite shut, which was odd, considering it was not a very warm afternoon. I could see Lady Hindon, side view, and it struck me that her head was bent far back over the top of the chair, as if she was about to have her hair washed. Didn't Dr. Mackeson mention this at all?"

"Not in my presence. Of course, he may have discussed it with Bruce, or made a mental note of it and decided not to mention it at all to anybody."

"He must have noticed it. He must have his suspicions. My guess is that he doesn't want to utter them unless he's absolutely forced to. I'm getting more and more sure, Paula, that this is going to be recorded as an accidental death, if not as natural death. Let's hope so, anyway. That lets us all out."

"I don't think it's so simple," said Paula, "but please finish your story. Did you see us come into the library?"

"I saw the door beginning to open, and then I thought I'd better go back to the front entrance and come in the proper way. But you do see that I would have had time to nip in and finish off the old girl and get out again through the window."

"Only just time," retorted Paula. "If this were a classic country-house whodunit you'd be a very marginal suspect. But it does show that somebody else could have got in—or got out—that way."

"Exactly. Ernest Brooker."

"Or Rupert Fisher."

"Or the statutory unknown."

"And Bruce Wiley," concluded Paula, "would not even have needed to come in or go out through the library window because he was in the house all the time, and I've only got Jill's word that he stood to gain nothing from Lady Hindon's death. If only we knew what was in her will."

"Mama is in the process of enquiring, and you and I will have to practice patience. How about a game of Scrabble?"

Paula at first rejected this suggestion. She was much too restless and anxious to be able to concentrate, but after a little more useless speculation, and some assurances from Andy that his mother would be very pleased to have her back, she decided that some harmless pastime was just what was needed, and they played until the cat woke up and demanded his dinner.

Three times during their game Andy had jumped up to answer the phone; twice it was a business call for Frances, quite unconnected with the events at Merle House, and the third time it was a colleague of Paula's, wanting to know in some detail about her recovery from the accident.

"I've got into a shocking state of nerves," said Paula when she replaced the receiver. "I keep imagining there's been another car crash."

"So do I."

"But why should there be?"

"Let's have some tea," said Andy abruptly.

Paula had not realized until that moment just how anxious he was himself. Of course it must be on account of his mother; of course the chances that Andy had actually gone into the library at Merle House were so small as to be barely perceptible, but nevertheless she wished he had not told her about that unlocked window. Frances and I did take quite a while to find our way along the corridor, she thought; and Bruce had certainly gone in the other direction, presumably towards the kitchen; and Andy didn't seem to want to be in the house, either before or after we found Lady Hindon dead.

Perhaps he had actually stepped inside the library. If he was anything like herself, books would draw him like a magnet.

"I do wish you hadn't proclaimed yourself a suspect," she said in what she intended to be a jokey manner as they sat down at the kitchen table.

Andy replied quite seriously, "Don't you think it's a good idea to widen the field? If Bruce and Jill are working hard to get Ernest accused of murder, then a little extra confusion might be helpful."

Paula leaned her head on her hand. "I wish I'd never listened to Jill."

"Don't say that. You've learned a lot. Here they are."

Paula jumped up. Andrew caught her arm. "Paula—Mama doesn't know that there is a possibility that Lady Hindon was killed. And Ernest doesn't know either. Unless he did it himself, of course."

"Okay. I'll be careful."

"Thanks."

Paula ran towards the front door. Frances greeted her without surprise and apparently without any recollection of the coolness that there had been between them.

"I'm so glad you're back," she said. "This is Ernest Brooker. Oh, of course you've met. I'd forgotten."

Paula shook hands with Frances's companion. A slightly built man, very upright, of medium height. White-haired. A scholarly face. An interesting face, with a remote, almost tireless look about it. He would fit well into a portrait gallery of poets and philosophers.

"I enjoyed your seminar," he was saying. "I thought you handled it very well. And at such short notice too."

"Thank you."

There was a moment's silence. We have all been talking and thinking so much about him, thought Paula, that it is quite disconcerting to meet him face to face. And he is terribly shy. It makes one shy too.

Frances was no help. She was, as Andy had said, very agitated, smiling at Ernest, going into the sitting-room and coming out again for no apparent reason, starting sentences and not finishing them.

"Oh—you're having tea—I think Ernest—we had tea— and we meant to go—you see, Paula, we got delayed by the lawyers, and Ernest's wife—"

She came into the kitchen and began to clear away the cups and plates from the table, suddenly stopped doing this, and opened a cupboard and looked inside it. It was obvious that she scarcely knew what she was doing.

Andrew took charge. He produced whisky for Ernest and sherry for his mother, and within ten minutes they were all sitting down in comfort and with at least an outward appearance of calmness. This boy, thought Paula, has an extraordinary capacity for organising things—and people—without appearing to do so. Great presence of mind and a lot of self-control. He ought to make use of these gifts. Unfortunately, the greater grew her own respect for Andrew's qualities, the more she began to think it not impossible that he could have seized the opportunity to come into the library at Merle House and hold the cushion over Lady Hindon's face. Speed of thought, speed of action, a casual, almost lazy manner, as if nothing very much was taking place—that was Andrew's way.

"We got so late," Frances was saying, "because Ernest wanted to go to the clinic. But Alice was very tired, so he didn't stay long, and I didn't go in to see her at all, so—"

"What they want to know," said Ernest, putting down his

glass and interrupting Frances, "is what Bernard Smith had to say." He looked at Paula and then at Andy and then at the floor. "She has left me nearly everything," he said very quietly. "Merle House and the bulk of the estate."

This is the first time, said Paula to herself, that I have ever been in company with somebody who has just inherited a fortune. How strange. No excitement or joy. He looks thoroughly depressed. Guilt? Shock? Worry at the responsibility?

"Everything, Merle House and all," repeated Frances, beginning to laugh. "Imagine that, Paula. Merle House! Don't you think Ernest will be a perfect owner of Merle House? I think he ought to turn it into an arts centre. There's that wonderful library, and rooms upstairs that will be ideal as studios for painters and sculptors, and the drawing-room would make a delightful music room—oh, Paula? Can't you see it? Don't you think it will be wonderful?"

She leaned over to take Paula's hand, spilling a little sherry on her skirt as she did so, and stared at her eagerly, almost imploringly. "Would you come and teach there, Paula? Wouldn't you like to?"

"It sounds an excellent idea," said Paula. "Is that what you are thinking of doing, Ernest?"

"It's much too early to think of doing anything," he replied. "I don't even know that I can accept this legacy. I feel" —he paused as if searching for the right words—"very far from happy about it."

"But why, dearest, why?" Frances let go of Paula and turned to face him. "She meant you to have it. She's always wanted you to have it. She's nobody else to leave it to."

"If she had wanted to endow an arts centre she would have appointed trustees to carry out her wishes," said Earnest.

"But she didn't. She wanted you to do it," said Frances very emphatically, and Paula had the impression that this argument had been going on ever since the visit to the lawyer's office, and that it was gaining fresh momentum in the presence of the audience of herself and Andy.

"She wanted me to think I was going to have it," amended Ernest. "That's a very different thing. I hope you don't think," he added, turning to the others, "that my friendship with Lady Hindon was based purely on my calculation of eventual benefit to myself. I have known her for very many years, from long before she married Sir Reginald."

"Yes, yes," said Frances impatiently. "Andrew and Paula know all about it. Everybody knows how tremendously loyal you have been to her. Nobody could possibly believe that you were just hoping for an inheritance."

"That is where we differ, my dear. Most people would believe just that."

Paula glanced at Andy, and he gave her a warning look, as if to say: Don't speak, let them get on with it. But it seemed as if Ernest, at any rate, was tired of the argument, for he turned to Andrew and said, "Please don't think that I'm not grateful for your mother's enthusiasm. Of course I've got hopes and dreams of my own. How could I help but have them? But I feel so shocked and upset, and the whole situation is so confused and so uncertain, that I don't feel able to give way to these hopes and dreams just yet. We don't even know how Lady Hindon died. There seems to be a distinct possibility that she willed her own death."

Silence followed this statement. Paula, mindful of Andy's warning, dared not speak. Andy was looking at his mother, and Frances was looking at Ernest with a mixture of pride and affection and concern.

"I suppose that means," said Andy at last, "that there will have to be an inquest."

"Yes," said Ernest, "there will certainly have to be an inquest."

# ———16———

Paula heard this with a sickening sense of apprehension. So it was not all over, bar the rumours and the gossip. There was to be no easy way out. She would have to stand up in public and describe how she had found Lady Hindon dead. If she were to be completely honest, she would also have to describe how she had noticed the orange cushion, and how she had been struck by the position of the head. But she need not mention her theories. Coroners' enquiries were designed to elicit facts, not theories, from witnesses. She would tell the truth, exactly as she had told it to Dr. Mackeson; she need say no more.

She had been deep in her own thoughts and had missed something that one of the others had said. Andy was looking at her warningly again.

"It was that stuff of Melanie's," said Frances. "I knew it was from the first."

"It certainly seems to have been partly responsible," agreed Ernest. "At any rate, in view of the results of the postmortem, Dr. Mackeson felt unable to sign a certificate stating the cause of death. So Bernard Smith told us."

"It was an accident, of course," said Frances. "I'm sure she didn't kill herself."

"Did Bernard Smith know any more?" asked Andy.

"If he did," replied Ernest, "he didn't tell us. He hoped I would appreciate that no action could be taken in the matter of

Lady Hindon's estate until the cause of death had been determined, and I replied that this would give me a chance to think over my own attitude towards the legacy."

"There ought not to be any thinking over," cried Frances. "You must take it, Ernest. There's no question of anything else. When I think how that woman has treated you—excuse me." She got rather unsteadily to her feet. "I'm not feeling very well."

She hurried out of the room and they could hear her going upstairs. Paula made a move as if to follow, but Ernest restrained her.

"She isn't ill," he said. "Just very overwrought. Best let her recover at her own pace. I ought to be going. Is there anything else I can tell you? I'm afraid you've been having an anxious time, Andrew. But it's a great relief to me to know that you are here to look after your mother."

He paused a moment before going on. "What is particularly upsetting her is the fact that I actually went to see Lady Hindon yesterday afternoon. At about two-thirty. At her own urgent request. She telephoned me at lunchtime and said she had something very important to tell me. She sounded worried, almost frightened, but of course I don't know whether that was genuine or assumed. She has always been a very good actress."

"Did she say what it was about?" asked Andy.

"No. Only that it was very urgent, and that she would rather nobody else knew that I was coming. She would leave the library window open, she said, and I could come in that way. I said I would much prefer to come to the front door as usual, but in the end she became so upset that I was obliged to agree. In fact I debated for some while whether I should go at all. I'd had this sort of phone call before."

Another pause. When he went on it was obvious that he was finding it difficult to speak. "You will be hearing this from another quarter, I have no doubt, so I had better tell you myself. Lady Hindon has been in the habit of telling me, with great ceremony, that I was to benefit under her will, and on other occasions of telling me, with equal ceremony, that she had changed her mind. I have put up with this—shall we say—cat-and-mouse treatment for some years, largely for Frances's sake. But it has become increasingly distasteful, and on the previous occasion—when she informed me that I was to be disinherited—I very nearly did not go. I had no idea whether she ever carried out her threats or her promises. It was only this afternoon that I learned from Bernard Smith that in fact she usually did."

"So you did go the previous time, and she told you that you were to be out of the will?" said Andy.

"Yes. That was about two months ago. It came more as a relief than a disappointment. Ever since then I have been making up my mind that if ever I received another such summons I should not respond to it, even if it resulted in a complete breach with Lady Hindon and great distress for Frances, not to mention the loss of an inheritance."

He smiled faintly. "I can pretend that this didn't weigh with me at all, but I truly believe, Andrew, that the thought of your mother weighed even more. You can see why we are so at odds with each other now. Anyway, in the end I weakened, as usual, and drove over to Merle House after lunch. Alice was in hospital and I was on my own. We have a daily woman who doesn't come at weekends, but sometimes leaves me a meal to heat up. I got to Merle House at about twenty to three and decided, in a silly little gesture of defiance, that I would not follow the instructions to come to the library window, but that I would ring the bell. Bruce took a long time to let me in, and looked not at all pleased when he saw me.

"I explained that Lady Hindon had asked me to come, and he said she was in the library as usual, and I said he didn't need to come with me and I was sorry to have disturbed him. He muttered something about cricket, and went away. I knocked on the library door and got no answer, tried again with the same result. I was just about to try the door and then I suddenly thought, no, why not go to the window. If she is asleep, I shall disturb her by opening the door, but if I go round to the window I can probably see from there. And if she is asleep, I shall simply go away. That lets me out.

"You will no doubt think this cowardly, but I was in the state to snatch at any excuse to avoid the interview. So I went back along the corridor to the hall. There was no sign of Bruce, nor any sound at all in the house. I let myself out at the front door, and walked along to the library window. It's only a few yards along the terrace."

"I know," put in Andy.

"The sun was shining on the windows and into the room, and I could see inside quite clearly. She was sitting in her chair, facing the fireplace, with her handbag hanging from the arm of the chair. I could not see her face, but she was leaning back as if she was fast asleep. I thought, Thank God, at least I am spared this interview, and I came away and drove home."

"You didn't go in at all then?" asked Andy.

"No indeed. That might have disturbed her."

"Nor try the window?"

"No, I didn't try the window. I just wanted to get away."

"I'm only asking," said Andy, "because it happens that I was doing very much the same thing about an hour later. My mother told you about how she and Paula found Lady Hindon, but I didn't tell my mother that I actually walked round to the library window myself and looked in. And I found it unlocked. So you see she really had left it open for you."

"Unless somebody opened it in the meantime," said Ernest.

"True," agreed Andy. "It's a pity we don't know whether it was open when you saw her."

"I don't see that it matters." Ernest stood up. "It doesn't make any difference to the drugs she had taken. I'll just go up and say goodbye to your mother, and then I must go."

After he had left the room, Paula looked enquiringly at Andy.

"I don't know," he muttered in reply to her unspoken question. "For Mama's sake I have to try to believe—but all the same, I don't know."

"Neither do I," said Paula.

The moment she had spoken she wished she had not said it, even to Andy. She did not want any doubts of Ernest to take possession of her mind. But his motive for wishing Lady Hindon dead was so very strong. Her tyranny over him was making his life a misery; she stood in the way of a happy relationship with Frances which would very probably, since Ernest's wife seemed to be failing rapidly, soon lead to their marriage. And if added to this was the fact that Ernest knew she was about to revoke a will that had been made in his favour. . .

Please, oh please let the death be by accident, prayed

Paula, and she began to dread the evening with Frances and to wonder how she was to keep up the pretense of believing in Ernest's innocence.

It turned out to be less difficult than she had feared. Frances, who calmed down a lot when Ernest was out of the house, talked incessantly about the plans for a Merle House arts centre, and needed only encouragement and an occasional murmur of appreciation from Paula. Andy left them to it and went off on his own.

The following morning Frances announced that she would be busy most of the day. There was her class in Salisbury, and she wanted to spend as much time as possible with Ernest. Could Paula amuse herself?

This suited Paula very well. "I'll see if Rupert has got back from London," she said. "He invited me to lunch when I met him yesterday morning."

"Where did you meet him?" asked Frances, but she was not really interested, and scarcely listened to Paula's reply. We are growing apart, Frances and I, thought Paula sadly but without any of the intensity of hurt and resentment that she had felt before. It was as if that immature part of herself that had looked up to Frances as a mentor and as an ideal, had at last grown up, and wanted only that Frances should come through her present difficulties into a happy and rewarding future.

Rupert answered her phone call. He would be delighted to see her. But he would not be alone. Melanie was coming to lunch too. She was deeply distressed about Lady Hindon's death, and the part that she herself played in it.

"Then she will want to talk to you without me being there," said Paula.

"On the contrary. She will be mightily relieved to see you. You'll be able to answer some of her questions. Have the police been in touch with you, by the way?"

"No, not yet."

"Then they soon will be. But try not to worry. It really is just a matter of routine preparation for the inquest. Poor Paula. You've got Gloria's as well. But with any luck, they'll be at the same sitting. This is quite a law-abiding and peaceful neighbourhood on the whole, so there's not usually much of a waiting-list for the coroner's services. Why don't you phone the Inspector yourself? I can give you the phone number."

Paula thanked him, and after Frances had gone, she made the call. An appointment was fixed for the following morning, and she was told that the two inquests would almost certainly take place on the same day, probably in about a week's time.

Then she went out to find Andy, who was lying on his back on the ground under the old blue Vauxhall, with only his feet visible.

He wriggled out and swore at the car.

"Can I give you a lift?" asked Paula after she had told him her news.

"No thanks. I'm determined not to be beaten. I'm up to here"—and he put an oily finger to his chin—"with human emotions, and it's quite a relief to kick a heap of old metal about."

Paula left him to it. There was plenty of time before she need set out for her lunch date, for Rupert lived in the village of Merle itself, a few miles beyond Merle House, and barely half an hour's drive from Winsford, but she felt too restless to stay in Brookside Cottage. For the first time since the car crash her headache had gone away completely, and she began to realise just how much her own feelings and thoughts and actions during the last few days had been affected by the shocked and nervous condition she had been in.

Today she could look with some detachment at the people and the situations with which she had become involved. She cared a great deal about Frances; she liked and admired Andrew; she liked Rupert, had mixed feelings about Ernest, had been fascinated by Lady Hindon, disliked Bruce Wiley and was alternately attracted and repelled by Jill. The other people whom she met aroused no very strong reactions, and she knew she would forget them as soon as she returned to her own life.

Paula got into the mini and drove away with no particular destination in mind. It was another bright, crisp autumn morning, and it was pleasant to dawdle along the lanes, pulling out of the way whenever a faster and more purposeful vehicle came up behind her.

When she came to a cross-roads she took the turning which led to Merle House. If the gates were open, she would drive in. If Bruce saw her she could say she happened to be passing and it occurred to her to stop and ask how Jill was and to apologise for deserting her yesterday. He would not believe her, but it didn't matter. They were firmly in opposite camps now—Bruce and Jill on the one hand, Frances and Ernest on the other—and Paula had thrown in her lot with Frances and Ernest.

The gates were open, and she turned the mini into the drive. There seemed to be nobody about and she drove on up to the house and parked in the same place as on her first visit. There was no other car to be seen. Bruce's must be in the garage; or in use. Paula sat for a minute or two looking around her and seeing the whole place with Frances's eyes.

It would indeed be a very suitable spot for some sort of adult-education college or as a haven for writers and artists. At one time Lady Hindon herself seemed to have been interested in the idea. If only she had been of a different character —a benevolent despot, not a malicious one.

But had she really been so bad?

Paula tried to sort out what she had seen for herself of Lady Hindon from what people had told her. On the whole, her own impression had been of a very tough and clever woman who got her own way, but not of an intrinsically vicious woman. That impression had come from others: from Frances and Ernest who feared her; from Jill who hated her. Perhaps the truth was to be found somewhat nearer to Rupert's more charitable attitude. Perhaps, in her deep unhappy loneliness, she had deliberately taken doses of drugs that she hoped would kill her.

It would be good to talk to Rupert about it. He would give a much more balanced view than any of the others.

Paula got out of the car and walked towards the house. While she was here, she might as well check up on what Andrew had said about the library window.

The library would be in the left-hand wing of the house, a long rectangular room. Between that and the front entrance, which itself formed a sort of wing, was the large drawing-room in which Frances and Paula had been brought tea by the maid, Mrs. Carson.

Yes, Andy was quite right. If one walked across the court-yard from the front doorstep, one would be at the library window much more quickly than if one went indoors and along the corridors, which involved passing through several doors and turning corners.

After walking across the courtyard, Paula stood by the long window and looked into the library. The windows were locked, but she could see quite clearly into the room. It looked exactly the same as when she had found Lady Hindon dead, except that the wheel-chair had been removed.

She stood there for some time, thinking, wondering, and remembering, and was just about to turn away when she was startled to hear a male voice just behind her.

"There's nobody at home and it's all locked up. You can't get in."

It was a young voice, not particularly friendly, but very sure of itself.

"So I see," said Paula, recovering from her surprise. "I'd hoped to find Mr. Wiley. Are you wanting to see him too?"

The boy stared at her. He was of medium height, of unremarkable appearance, wearing very dirty jeans and carrying a spade.

"You must be Terry," said Paula, indirectly answering her own question. "Terry Carson. I met your mother here the other day."

"She told me. I knew it was you. What do you want?"

"To ask Mr. Wiley something, but since he doesn't seem to be here, I can't do it."

"What did you want to ask him?"

"Why do you ask me that, Terry?" countered Paula.

There was a silence while they stared at each other, summing each other up. Paula had the feeling that the boy was wanting to tell her something, but could not quite make up his mind to do so. For her part, she did not feel inclined to put much trust in him. Mrs. Carson had seemed to be a competent and reliable person, but the son did not make so favourable an impression. Paula searched her mind for Frances's remarks about him when explaining that he worked for Mrs. Barton next door. Not much of a gardener, but a bit of a con-man, Frances had said.

Presumably he was still helping in the grounds at Merle House, and therefore had a right to be here, but from where they stood there was visible only the expanse of lawn in front of the house and the beech trees that bordered it on the far side. Where would Terry be needing to use a spade?

She asked this question aloud. Let him think her nosey. If he had a guilty conscience he would be only too eager to give innocent explanations of himself.

"We're digging a new flower-bed," he replied, jerking his head over his shoulder to indicate the area beyond the library wing. "Mr. Wiley said the job was to go on. My mate'll be along later."

"I see," said Paula. "I've never seen the gardens. There don't seem to be any flowers here in front."

"They're round the back. She liked to keep it that way," said Terry. "Didn't want anything in front of the house. She said it would spoil the line of it."

"Yes. Yes, it would," said Paula thoughtfully. "Did you ever see Lady Hindon yourself?" she went on.

"Only when she came outdoors. I've never been in the house."

"What did you think of her?"

Terry seemed to be deciding first what he thought of Paula before he answered.

"She was a poor old cow," he said at last. "Why was they all so scared of her? A puff of wind would've knocked her over. I could've done it myself with one hand."

"Done it yourself?" asked Paula sharply. "What are you talking about, Terry?"

"I'm talking about what you want to know, ain't I? There's my mate coming. We'll be getting on with the job. It's no use you waiting here for Mr. Wiley. Not unless you want to stay here for hours and hours."

And he winked at Paula and disappeared round the corner of the building, leaving her with a completely different train of thought to follow, and with a strong inclination to go after him and see what he and his mate were doing.

Was there perhaps some way of getting into the house? It looked very unguarded and exposed, almost an invitation to burglars. Presumably there was some sort of security arrangement, though she could see no sign of any burglar alarm. No doubt Lady Hindon might have thought they would spoil the line of the house.

Terry's view of her as a "poor old cow" was very different from that of everybody else. He was evidently not impressed by all the outward paraphernalia of wealth and social superiority, and saw only the extreme physical weakness. A variation on the old fable of the emperor's new clothes.

A sick and suffering old woman. Very lonely. But surely if she had decided to kill herself she would have made certain of doing the job properly? Unless she had wanted somebody to be blamed for it. Vengeance from beyond the grave. This seemed not impossible, but then Paula recollected that the most likely person to be blamed was Melanie King, who was surely the least likely person for Lady Hindon to wish to harm.

As she was thinking, Paula was walking slowly in the direction that Terry had taken. Beyond the house was a high beech hedge, with a gap in it leading to a shrubbery. Here Paula hesitated a moment. She did not want to play hide-and-seek with Terry and his mate in this maze of bushes and bushes, and it was in any case getting too late to linger. But curiosity was strong. In the end she compromised by walking a little way along the path nearest to the side of the house. There were no windows here on the ground floor, and only small windows above. The building looked stark and forbidding.

She went on, unable to stop herself, but feeling nervous and apprehensive, until the path began to widen and she could see further ahead to what looked like a kitchen garden. There was a line of tall sticks supporting runner beans, a few late sunflowers, and an apple tree within her line of vision. Beyond were the high beeches that half circled Merle House at the back and at the far side—the start of the beechwoods that covered the further hill.

Paula stood still, thinking again of Frances's dream. What a happy and fruitful place this could be. She saw it filled with painters and writers and musicians and nature-lovers and gardeners of all ages: a community of all that was hopeful and creative and beauty-loving in human beings.

This was no sudden idea of Frances and Ernest's. They must have long talked of it, have yearned for it. And only one frail old woman, whom Terry could have "done with one hand," stood in the way.

They had planned it together. It was their hope, their

dream, their gift to themselves and to the future. Of this Paula had now no doubts at all. Only one question remained: Had Ernest, seeing the vision about to be snatched from him, made sure that he would not lose it; and if so, had anybody seen him, was there any proof?

# 17

Rupert Fisher's cottage was rather similar to Frances's, but even more cluttered. It seemed that he shared Frances's passion for gardening, and Paula arrived to find him and Melanie King discussing the best time to take up dahlias. He left them together in the little sitting-room while he disappeared to attend to the meal, but Paula felt quite unable to continue the conversation.

From plants, however, it was only a short step to herbal medicines, and Melanie was only too anxious to talk about the subject that was filling her mind.

"My friend who prescribed the mixture for me," she explained to Paula, "is a qualified medical practitioner as well as a qualified herbalist, and I have found it very useful myself for relieving pain as well as for a sedative."

"Is it dangerous?" asked Paula. "I mean, would it be easy to take too much without realising?"

"Henbane, or 'hyoscyamus niger' to give it the correct name, is of course a poison," replied Melanie, "but it would take a very large dose to be lethal to an adult human being. There is not the slightest danger in taking the correct dose, or even in taking more than prescribed."

"So if one wanted to poison somebody—or to kill oneself in this way—one would not choose henbane?"

"No indeed. Most certainly not. One would choose perhaps

aconite. Or belladonna. But you know, Dr. Glenning, it is really not at all easy to be sure of poisoning anybody. People do not understand, they do not understand at all how very carefully controlled herbal medicines are, and how very skilled and experienced the practitioners. Properly used, but of course if people deliberately abuse them—"

Here Melanie, who had been growing more and more agitated as she talked, had to break off to recover herself.

Paula made sympathetic murmurs, and eventually Melanie went on.

"Where I do blame myself most bitterly is that I did not persuade Lady Hindon to see my friend and let him prescribe for her. It was terribly wrong of me to hand on to another person a medicine that had been prescribed only for myself. Very wrong indeed."

Paula protested that people were doing this all the time. She herself had more than once begged a couple of sleeping pills off a friend to ensure a good night's rest before an exam. Melanie really must not blame herself like this.

"I don't think Lady Hindon ought to have asked you," she concluded. "If she wanted to try herbal medicines, she ought to have consulted the expert herself. Had she ever asked you for anything before?"

This produced a spate of words in defence of Lady Hindon: She disliked and distrusted doctors, and could never find one who really understood her. She, Melanie, could well appreciate this. Lady Hindon had suffered a very great deal, far more than most people realised, but Melanie had understood and pitied her.

"But surely you warned her," began Paula, but got no further.

"Of course I warned her!" cried Melanie. "I told her again and again that on no account must she take Dr. Mackeson's tablets as well as my drops. It must be one or the other. She must not, simply must not, mix them. That could be fatal. Of course I warned her. But it seems that she ignored my warning. Oh, I have been so wrong! I ought never to have done it."

Paula, doing her best to soothe Melanie, wished that Rupert would return. He was much better at this sort of thing than she was. Perhaps, after all, it had not been any kindness to encourage Melanie to talk about her problems.

"If it does turn out," she said carefully, "that the mixture of drugs did kill Lady Hindon, would you be subject to any penalty?"

"Not exactly a penalty," was the reply, "but you can imagine, Dr. Glenning, the sort of things that will be said about me."

And in a voice barely audible she added, "I am sure somebody has told you about my sister."

"Yes. I am very sorry. I can well appreciate how you feel about this."

"Lady Hindon suffered so much, and she was so very brave."

Melanie got up from the chair in which she was sitting and began to rearrange the collection of china dogs that stood on a shelf near the fireplace. Her voice became more and more agitated, her movements more and more jerky and nervous.

"Lady Hindon did not want to die. All she wanted was some relief from the pain and discomfort. She wanted peace. She wanted peace!" Melanie's voice rose to hysteria. Paula tried her best to calm her but without much success, and it was a very great relief when Rupert came in and announced that lunch was ready.

Melanie became quieter when she saw him, and she actually ate quite a lot of the excellent chicken casserole that he had made. Paula noted that he kept the conversation on the subject of Lady Hindon's death, but tried to take it out of the realm of Melanie's fears and guilt and to see it from the other points of view.

This seemed to help Melanie, but when the talk turned to an inevitable discussion of who was likely to gain by Lady Hindon dying, Paula had to be very careful what she said. Of course they knew about the legacy to Ernest, but to her relief they appeared to know nothing about Ernest's visit to Merle House that afternoon.

"There couldn't be a more worthy inheritor," said Rupert. "Ernest will make excellent use of Merle House."

"Indeed he will," echoed Melanie.

Paula agreed, but to herself she was saying, Ernest's visit is known to himself and to Frances, and to me and Andy, and to Bruce and Jill. That's quite a lot of people. Three of them can be trusted to keep silent; two of them most certainly cannot be, unless . . .

Unless they can see some advantage to themselves in keeping the knowledge a secret. Could that be what Bruce and Jill were up to? Waiting until Lady Hindon's death was recorded as accidental or suicide or even by natural causes, and then blackmailing Ernest?

The idea took possession of Paula's mind, and caused her to miss the first part of something that Rupert was saying, but when he repeated it she was startled out of her abstraction.

"Mrs. Carson is worried about Terry. She says he is always inclined to be rather sly—my word, not hers, she is very loyal to her son—and it has been particularly bad this last couple of days. Since Lady Hindon died, in fact. She doesn't know whether he really knows something that he isn't telling, or whether he is just making a big drama of it all."

"Terry Carson," said Paula. "I saw him at Merle House. On my way here."

"Whatever were you doing at Merle House?" asked Melanie.

"Just killing time. It was one of those sudden impulses," added Paula, seeing that Melanie still looked surprised and even a little displeased. "It had all been so horrible there that afternoon, that when I found myself in the neighbourhood I thought I would like to have a look at it in peace. With nobody there."

She stopped abruptly, conscious that she was doing too much explaining.

"But there wasn't nobody there. Bruce is in residence," said Melanie. "Did you want to see him?"

"I don't really know. Perhaps I did. Anyway, he wasn't in," went on Paula more briskly. "I ran into Terry Carson in the courtyard and he told me that the place was all locked up and that he and his mate were digging a flower-bed behind the shrubbery. He'd got a spade with him. It—this sounds awfully silly—it gave me a slight shock. I suppose my mind was running on deaths and funerals and graves."

There was a short silence, broken eventually by Rupert.

"Lady Hindon will be buried in the parish churchyard. Next to her husband. There is no chapel at Merle House. I imagine it will be a very quiet ceremony. Unless some of her husband's business associates feel they ought to come and pay their respects. There are very few relatives. Only distant cousins."

Paula mentally thanked him for these remarks. Yet again he had succeeded in bringing their thoughts away from the realms of fantasy and conjecture and back to ordinary everyday life. Nevertheless, she was very interested in what Rupert had said about Terry.

"I'm afraid I did a bit of trespassing," she said. "I walked round towards the back of the house, just to see where the flower-beds could be."

"Beyond the shrubbery," said Rupert. "I expect they were digging in the vegetable garden. Perhaps some of it is to be turned over to flowers. They grow sweet peas and roses and chrysanthemums to provide decoration for the house, but there are very few ornamental beds at Merle."

"Has Terry got a mate?" asked Paula.

"Not really. It would be Bert Ford. He's actually in charge of the grounds. But Terry would hate to have to call him the boss."

"Do they work there every day?"

"Bert does. More or less full time. It's a big place to keep up, even with a gardening firm brought in to cut the grass. I don't know how long Terry spends. He certainly does other jobs as well."

"Frances's neighbour is one," said Paula. "That's when I first heard of him. Apparently he has defects as a gardener but is good at making people think he knows his job."

Rupert laughed. "That's Terry. He wanted to come over and dig my little patch—they live just down the road here, you know—but I wasn't having it. Oh well, if people are foolish enough to be taken in by him."

"But you don't think he's actually dishonest?"

"If he is, he's never been found out. No, I wouldn't think he goes in for such things as petty theft. He's got too high an opinion of himself. But if he saw a really big chance, then I think he would be tempted," concluded Rupert.

Paula remembered these words. The conversation moved on to Bruce, and here Paula told herself to be careful, not to give away anything that she had learned from Jill. From Rupert's and Melanie's remarks, she gathered that the relationship with Bruce was not generally known. Certainly neither of them seemed to have guessed at it. Bruce and Jill had been luckier than Frances and Ernest; or perhaps they had been cleverer.

Melanie wondered what Bruce would do now that he had lost both his job and his home and had, as far as was known, received no acknowledgment of his services in the will. Rupert's opinion was that Bruce had no cause to complain; he was sure that Sir Reginald, who had brought him to Merle in the first place, would have made sure that he would not lose when Lady Hindon died.

But would he gain, wondered Paula. It did not seem that he was to gain financially, but of course he would now be free to marry Jill and share with her River View and Gloria's money.

If this was what he wanted, then it seemed an agreeable enough future. They would certainly be comfortable, but in comparison with the inheritance of Merle House and the Hindon fortune, it was peanuts. Surely it was not enough to kill for. If this was all Bruce wanted, why could he not simply tell Lady Hindon that he was leaving her?

"I wonder that Bruce stayed at Merle for so long," said Paula aloud, "with such a difficult employer."

"I believe that Sir Reginald's provision for him was dependent on his remaining at Merle House during the lifetime of the widow," said Rupert. "I seem to remember a discussion with Norman and Bernard Smith when they were both here one evening. We were talking about the rights and wrongs of people trying to control other people's lives after their own death. You know the sort of thing. I bequeath such and such to my daughter provided she does not marry a particular person whom I happen to dislike. It can be done out of pure spite, and the courts don't look favourably upon such cases. But Bernard pointed out that a testator may act in very good faith, purely to protect the interests of somebody who will need such protection.

"He didn't mention any names, but I am sure he had Sir Reginald Hindon in mind. Knowing how difficult it was for his wife to keep on good terms with the people who were serving her, he may well have decided that a conditional legacy to the one person who seemed able to cope was the best way to ensure that she and Merle House were looked after. That's my opinion, at any rate."

The others agreed that it sounded very likely, and Paula was left asking herself whether this would increase Bruce's motive for wishing Lady Hindon dead. On the surface, it appeared that it would. So long as she lived, he was tied to Merle House. But on the other hand she could not rid herself of the idea that Bruce, like Terry the gardener, was not interested in small benefits. If Sir Reginald's provision for him was adequate, but not over-generous, then Bruce might well prefer to stay in his present position in the hope of getting more out of Lady Hindon eventually, in which aim he would probably be abetted by Jill.

Rupert's remarks were very interesting, and they filled in some more pieces of the jigsaw puzzle, but on the whole they did not alter the main picture. They made no difference to the fact that Ernest Brooker had an overwhelming motive for wishing Lady Hindon to die at the very moment when she had done so.

They moved back into the little sitting-room for their coffee after lunch, and both Rupert and Melanie began to ask Paula questions about her own life and work.

"I shall go home tomorrow afternoon," she said presently. "I've got another week's leave, but I feel so much better now that I'd like to start getting back to normal. In any case I'll have to come down again at the end of next week for the inquest."

"Oh, that inquest." Melanie shuddered. "How I dread it."

Rupert did his reassuring act. They seemed to have come full circle, and shortly afterwards Paula got up to go.

"I'm supposed to be resting in the afternoons," she said, "and as I've been quite ignoring medical instructions up till now . . ."

The farewells were very friendly, accompanied by promises to keep in touch. Paula did not feel that she had been anything but a welcome guest, but nevertheless she knew that they were going to talk about her a great deal after she had gone, and she had a sudden vision of all these little circles of talk going on all over the neighbourhood, all over every neighbourhood, all the time. A and B and C talk about D and E. But when only A and B are present, then they talk about C, who in turn talks with F, and so on in an infinite number of combinations and permutations.

Like mathematical sets, overlapping each other in places, and in other places standing on their own, as the innermost heart of the human creature stands alone.

The geometry of human relationships. In this particular exercise, Merle House was the master set, containing all the others.

Paula expanded on this analogy in her mind as she drove slowly back to Winsford. She herself was, mentally at least, beginning to drift out of the Merle House set and back into her London life. Tomorrow evening would see her completely absorbed into the latter. She would come down for the inquests, and after that it was not very likely that she would visit Frances again.

Not in similar circumstances, at any rate. If all went well for Frances and Ernest, then perhaps some time in the future she might be invited to teach a literature course at Merle House College. At the moment she felt she would not want to accept—it would be impossible ever to still her own suspicions. And it would be much better, now, if she and Frances were to drift apart, as they seemed already to be doing, without any animosity, just in the natural course of events.

There was nobody in at Brookside Cottage when Paula got back, but a note addressed to her lay on the telephone table in the hall.

"Mama won't be back tonight," it said. "She is staying— guess where?—but I shall be here about five o'clock. Do you want to be entertained? Theatre in Salisbury? Dinner? More Scrabble? Or a quiet evening with the telly? See you soon. Love, Andy."

Paula smiled and made her choice without any hesitation at all. The house felt cosy and welcoming. Leslie, somewhat neglected by his owner during the last few days, came to sit on her lap and purr, and she watched a television programme that gave items of local interest. It was salutary to find that there was plenty going on in the southwestern counties of England that had nothing to do with the affairs at Merle House.

Stonehenge, for example. Somebody wanted to build a three-storey restaurant by the car park, and people were protesting that it would spoil the view. A rare type of wading bird had been spotted in the estuary of the River Severn, and the enthusiasts had been assembling in hordes on the spot.

Poor bird, thought Paula; better to be something commonplace and disregarded, like a sparrow.

When Andy came back twenty minutes later, the screen was full of cartoon figures whizzing around and exploding and vanishing, accompanied by a variety of squeaks and grunts and growls. Paula did not appear to notice them. She was fast asleep, curled up in the chair in her dark blue trousers and pale blue sweater, with her head turned towards the cushion and the cap of fair hair falling over her face. The marmalade cat, also asleep, sprawled half on Paula's knees and half on the arm of the chair.

To the onlooker she looked young and vulnerable and trusting. Perhaps too trusting.

Paula stirred, coming slowly to full consciousness.

"Apple tree," she murmured. "I was dreaming about ladders in apple trees."

"Nice dream?"

"Sort of. Like my grandmother's market garden. One of my favourite haunts when I was young." She sat up, clutching the cat, who protested loudly. "But it was menacing too, in my dream. It's nice to see you, Andy. Thanks for your note."

"Have you decided how you want to be entertained?"

"Yes. In no way at all. I shall watch 'Dallas' and go early to bed."

"I shall do likewise. I've been driving Toby and Liz around most of the day and have had enough. Sherry, Paula?"

"Thanks."

"I don't know if you are still interested in the death of Gerald Alexander," said Andrew presently. "Toby and Liz were talking about it again. They'd come to the conclusion that the drowning really was a genuine accident."

"Jill told me that she had firm evidence that Gloria had fixed it," said Paula.

"Did you believe her?"

"I don't know. Jill Freebody has got a very nasty, sick sense of humour. I believe she enjoys making outrageous statements in such a way that people think they can't possibly be true, and then they do turn out to be true after all. There's only two things about Jill that I really feel sure of, and one is that she loves cooking and the other is that she loves Bruce."

"Two ruling passions. Can she then really be so bad?"

"I don't know. At the moment I'm too lazy to care. Have you got a ruling passion, Andy?"

Rather to Paula's surprise, he took this question seriously, and for a long time they talked about Andy's great love, a Nigerian girl whom his mother had met once and did not like. Worlds away from Merle House: a completely different human set.

# 18

Paula's visit to the police station turned out to be very much a matter of routine. P.C. Grover, who had called on her about the road accident in which she had been injured, took down her statement concerning the discovery of Lady Hindon, and the Inspector only appeared at the end of the interview.

Paula repeated exactly what she had said to Dr. Mackeson: that the eyes were open and staring and that the position of the head looked unnatural. She did not say anything about the crumpled cushion and her own theories, and nobody asked for her opinion. The Inspector thanked her for consenting to be a witness, and politely hoped that she had recovered from the car crash.

The drive into London felt endless and very exhausting, and it took even longer than usual to find a place to leave the car. Paula went straight to the nearest supermarket, knowing that once she had climbed the three flights of stairs to her own apartment she would never want to come out again today, and bought some essential supplies.

Only a couple of hours travel, she thought as she waited at the check-out, and yet it is a completely different world from the little Wiltshire villages. Plenty of brown and yellow faces, for example. In the countryside they had been all white. And nobody here knew you nor cared anything about you. You were simply another human obstacle blocking their way in the

160

bus queue, in the street, in the entrance to the shop.

To Paula it was familiar, even comforting. I could not live in a tight little rural community, she said to herself, where everybody knows everyone else's business. If the price to be paid is bouts of loneliness, then so be it.

But she was glad, nevertheless, to find on the doorstep the black cat who belonged to the girl in the ground-floor flat, waiting to be let in.

Its owner thanked Paula and they exchanged brief greetings.

"Been away?"

"Yes. In Wiltshire. Anything happened here?"

"Only more complaints from the basement that they can hear me walking about all night. You're lucky to have only deaf old Harry Perks under your flat."

Paula sympathised. "I should just ignore them."

"Don't worry. I will."

But I don't really know, said Paula to herself as she walked upstairs, whether in fact Alison does go to bed very late and disturb the neighbours. I don't know anything about her except that she's got a black cat and works at the B.B.C. And that if I were to fall downstairs and break my leg she would come and help me, as I would help her. And then we would go back to where we were before. Neighbours, not friends. That's how I want it.

Paula opened her own front door and was welcomed by the familiar muddle that she had left behind when she had responded to Frances's invitation. For about forty minutes she was happy reading the letters that had accumulated in her absence; making telephone calls; catching up with the college gossip; drinking coffee out of her favourite mug, a relic from childhood that had a gaudy picture of a teddy bear on one side; and letting the cigarette ash spill over the side of the ashtray without having to worry that anybody would comment on it.

And then suddenly, almost from one second to the next, her contentment vanished. Try as she would, she could not get the affairs of Merle House out of her mind. She had believed herself to be running away from them, but it seemed as if she had brought the puzzle back to London with her. It looked different at this distance, and she felt that she was tantalisingly close to seeing a different pattern. Not the pattern that had been dominating her mind and greatly distressing her ever since Jill Freebody had told her of Ernest Brooker's visit to Lady Hindon on the afternoon of her death. There were the same ingredients, but they needed shaking up a little to rearrange them. Like a Chinese puzzle. But she needed a little more information, and also another opinion. If only she could have had a chance to talk to Rupert on his own yesterday. If only they had not had to spend so much time trying to console Melanie. She felt sure that Rupert had an important clue; although he might not even know how important it was until he had linked it up with her own experiences. But she was not so sure, now that she had been thinking it over, that Rupert was unaware of the relationship between Frances and Ernest. He might well have been doing what Paula hoped she had successfully done herself: keeping absolutely quiet about it.

Rupert Fisher certainly liked to chat. One might even suspect him of being rather indiscreet, but Paula felt sure that if he really wanted to keep a secret he would do it more efficiently than many far more reserved people. And he must have been the confidant of many people both during his working life and after retirement. They would have been lucky to find such a listener—compassionate, tolerant, and trustworthy.

If only I could talk to Rupert, said Paula to herself. I am sure we could find out together what really happened at Merle House. At least we ought to be able to see clearly enough to prevent any further tragedy.

A further tragedy. It was this that was nagging at her mind. Ought she to give a warning? Ought she to alert somebody? She could certainly not drive back to Wiltshire again tonight. There was the telephone, of course, but was it wise to say this sort of thing over the wires?

Smoking one cigarette after another, she began to reproach herself for not having thought things through more carefully before she came away from Winsford. But it was only at a distance that she had begun to see clearly; she had needed to come away in order to do so.

Was she exaggerating the danger now? She thought perhaps that she was. After all, there was still a week before the inquest on Lady Hindon. Twice she picked up the telephone, only to replace the receiver before she had come to the end of the number. When at last she could bring herself to finish and to let it ring, there was no reply. Rupert Fisher was not at home. Why should he be? He was a sociable man; he had many friends and enjoyed other people's company.

Perhaps she had better talk to Andy. She called another number, but the telephone rang and rang in an empty house. Later, before she went to bed, she tried Rupert again, but there was no reply.

The following day she spent with friends, and managed not to think about Merle House for most of the time. When she returned home about five o'clock the telephone was ringing. It was Rupert Fisher himself, hoping he was not disturbing her.

"Not a bit," replied Paula. "I've been thinking about you all such a lot, and last evening I tried to speak to you."

"I'm sorry. I was over at Norman's. Hasn't Frances been in touch with you?"

"She called me late last evening to ask if I'd got home all right. We didn't talk for very long. She wasn't alone, and I don't think she was at home."

"I see. Then you won't have heard the news."

"News?"

"Yes. I'm extremely sorry to say, Paula, that—"

"—there's been another accident."

She completed his sentence so quickly that he sounded a little surprised when he continued.

"How did you guess? Or had you reasoned out that something like this was going to happen?"

"A mixture of both, I think. I've been terribly worried about it."

"Then you know who it was."

"I can guess. But please tell me, Rupert."

"Terry Carson, the gardening boy. He was found dead this morning at the foot of an apple tree in the vegetable garden at Merle House. Apparently he'd been up there pruning off the highest branches—it's a big old tree and some of them were dangerous. It looks as if he'd stepped off the ladder onto one of the rotten ones and come a-crash onto the cucumber frame beneath. He had severe head injuries."

There was silence on the line.

"Paula," said Rupert. "Paula, are you still there?"

"Yes. I'm still here. I believe I might perhaps have been able to prevent this."

"That makes two of us. Don't let's blame ourselves too much. It's more than likely that we couldn't have done anything, even if we had tried. But I think we ought to talk about it. Not on the phone, though. Could you face the prospect of coming down to Wiltshire again so soon? Or shall I get on the next train to London?"

"I'd rather come. We might be able to—to do something. Don't you think so, Rupert?"

"I'm glad you've said that. Would you like to stay here? The spare room is always ready, and I can meet any train you like in Salisbury. Or would you prefer to drive?"

"I'd rather drive. I'll be with you—let's see—at about nine o'clock?"

"Good girl. I'll have a meal ready. And I think perhaps we won't tell anybody that you are coming. Unless you feel you ought to call Frances?"

"Not if you think it better I don't. In any case she probably won't be in."

"I'll expect you at nine, then. Drive safely. Take care."

"And you take care too."

Paula did indeed take great care. Her mind was full of accidental deaths, booby-traps, and car-bombs. She checked the oil and tyres of the mini at the garage where it was serviced, and after the young assistant, whom she knew quite well, had filled the petrol tank, she asked him to look at the exhaust.

"It's making an awful noise. Many thanks, Bob."

The boy peered under the car and announced that he could find nothing wrong, and received a one-pound coin when Paula produced her credit card.

When she set off at last she told herself that it was absurd to imagine that somebody had followed her to London and done something lethal to her car as it stood in one of the side streets of Hampstead. There were no doubt people in Wiltshire who were very glad that she was out of the way, this inquisitive stranger whose arrival had, in a way, precipitated a chain of events. And those people would be far from pleased to find that she had come back.

But to track her down into her own life and try to ensure

that she did not return? Surely not. Nevertheless Paula took great care with her car, and drove with even more than the usual caution.

It had been dark for well over an hour when she reached the spot where only a week ago she had stopped to admire the splendours of the setting sun behind Stonehenge. She turned off at the same cross-roads. There was probably a quicker way to get to Merle village, but this was the road she knew best, and she did not feel like exploring unknown routes.

As she came near to the steep side lane that led up to the house that was, or would be, Jill's, she felt more and more tense and apprehensive. Was Jill fit to drive again by now? What car would she be using, if she were? And was she alone up there at River View? If not, who was with her? Mrs.— whatever the name of the woman was who had been coming to stay? Or Bruce?

There was no possible way in which somebody sitting in that bland showpiece of a house could see a yellow mini car passing along the road below. In fact one couldn't even see the road from River View.

Paula told herself this, but nevertheless she felt greatly relieved when she was well past the spot, and could see the lights of Winsford, half a mile on.

Here her anxiety was of a different kind, and a lot more rational.

Frances's cottage was in the centre of the village, quite a busy spot and very visible, even at night, because of the lights from the Shepherd's Rest. Both Frances and Andrew knew Paula's car well and would recognise it. Mrs. Barton next door would probably recognise it too.

It would have been better to avoid passing through Winsford. If somebody happened to be arriving at or departing from one of the cottages as she drove past, they would certainly see her. They might well notice even if they only happened to be glancing out of a window.

But it was too late to turn round, and in any case Paula was longing for the journey to end. So she drove on quickly, pretending that this was just another village that meant nothing to her, but of course she could not help glancing at Brookside Cottage as she came near it. There was no light to be seen in the house, and no car parked in the entrance. This should

perhaps have been reassuring, but Paula found that it set her
off worrying about Frances.

Was she with Ernest? Had she come out of her euphoric
dream into the cold light of reality? Had she begun to work
things out for herself? And what was Andy up to? Surely he
had not simply gone back to messing about in a used-car market in Salisbury and driving his friend Toby around?

There was no light in the neighbour's cottage either. Perhaps Mrs. Barton was visiting a friend and bemoaning the loss
of her gardener, Terry Carson.

Paula was glad to get away from the lights of Winsford and
into the winding lane beyond. But here other recollections
soon obtruded. Here was the dangerous corner where Jill had
swung the Mercedes off the road to try to avoid the oncoming
car. Here Gloria Alexander had had her fatal heart attack, and
Jill and Paula had received their injuries. It was good to get
away from this place too.

The trees grew close to the road; in the headlights of the
mini the trunks looked like ghosts.

Every few minutes Paula saw, with a mixture of relief and
apprehension, the lights of an oncoming car. Her sensations at
the time of the crash swept over her again. She was not yet
recovered from it. A lot more time must elapse before she
could once more drive around in the normal state of self-pre-
serving insensitivity.

When she came near to the gates of Merle House she began
to wish that she had accepted Rupert's offer to meet her at
Salisbury rail station. It would have been much more sensible
to sit in comfort and safety in a train full of business people
than to punish her nerves by driving alone along these dark
narrow lanes.

And yet this journey was serving a useful purpose. Paula
was very much getting the feel of the place again. From the
London commuter train she would have seen it with a sense of
detachment. Had she been sitting there reading of the three
deaths—Gloria, Lady Hindon, and Terry—she would not
have had any suspicions; she would have accepted that they
were either accidental or from natural causes. But driving
along the road to Merle, remembering so vividly her first im-
pressions of the people in the writing class, having lived with
Frances through her fears and hopes, having spent those

strange hours with Jill, and some rather pleasanter hours at Rupert's house, Paula felt herself deeply enmeshed in the web of fears and hopes and hatreds that were centered on Merle.

There must be no more accidents. That was why she was here. Rupert felt that too. It would be good to talk to him, absolutely freely this time. Together they would find the best way to bring this chain of events to an end. Perhaps he had some firm evidence, not merely hearsay or opinion, that they could take to the police. It would not be long now: she would soon be there.

But when she had passed the gates of Merle House and was driving the last mile toward the village of Merle, Paula was struck by yet another fear.

Supposing Rupert had not been cautious enough? Or supposing somebody had suspected that he knew or guessed too much?

He lived alone; he would take every possible care, but he might still be outwitted. There might yet be another accident. Supposing, when she arrived at Rupert's cottage in a few minutes' time, she was to find it in darkness, with no sign of life?

The thought was chilling. But it was succeeded by one that was even more so, one that Paula had at first reluctantly admitted, and had then shut her mind to.

On the afternoon of Lady Hindon's death, Rupert Fisher had driven Mrs. Carson round to the back entrance of Merle House, right round the far side of the building away from the road; had left her there with Bruce, and had then, so he said, driven straight home.

Paula had seen his car in the distance when she arrived there with Frances and Andy.

He had been on the spot at the vital time. If the library window had been unlocked, then he would have had access to the house. She knew no reason at all why he should wish to hasten Lady Hindon's death, except perhaps as a mercy killing, and she liked him very much indeed.

But if everybody was to be suspected, why should Rupert be immune?

Was his phone call what it seemed to be—a call for help in preventing further tragedy—or was it a trap into which Paula was so readily rushing?

When she was half a mile away from her destination Paula

said to herself: If it's a trap, at least I shall find out the truth.

When she was a quarter of a mile away, she said: If I can't trust Rupert, who then can I trust? Andy? But the same reasoning applied to him too. And he had got a motive of sorts: to protect his mother and ensure her future.

She turned a corner, drove the last few yards, and saw, standing in the roadway outside Rupert's cottage, just beyond the streetlamp, the battered old blue Vauxhall that Andy had been working on and had now got going again.

# 19

Andy opened the door to her.

"Hi, Paula. Rupert said you'd be coming. I've not been here long myself. Are you all right? Did you have a good drive down?"

He seemed anxious and nervous, speaking in short jerky sentences and unable to keep still. It was not like Andy to lose his cool. Paula felt fresh stabs of apprehension.

"Your mother—where is she? Is anything wrong?"

"She's at home. With Mrs. Barton. No. There's nothing exactly wrong. At least no more wrong than it was when you left. It's a pity she doesn't seem able to face realities, but then it could be a very big reality to have to face."

"What could be, Andy? What is all this? Where's Rupert?"

"He's making a phone call. He won't be long."

They moved into the little sitting-room. Paula put down her overnight bag and found a comfortable chair.

"Rupert called me in London," she said, "to tell me about Terry being killed by a fall. We didn't want to say anything much on the phone, but we agreed that it could not have been an accident and we thought we knew who was responsible. The idea was to decide whether we could do anything about it. That's how I come into this. How do you come into it, Andy?"

"In much the same way. When I heard about Terry I

reached the same conclusion. He'd been trying to blackmail whoever it was he saw in the library holding a cushion over Lady Hindon's face. Was that your conclusion, Paula?'"

"Yes, and I ought to have got to it much earlier. I ought to have begun to suspect after I had that talk with Terry, and when Rupert told me that Terry's mother was worried about him because he was in a very excited state and very secretive, I ought to have thought it through. But we were all rather preoccupied with Melanie and the drugs. I suppose that's why—"

Paula broke off.

"Partly why," said Andy, who seemed to be recovering his usual equanimity. "But I don't think it was the main reason for your omission. If indeed it was an omission."

Paula said nothing. She was leaning back in her armchair. She was very tired.

"This coffee's still good and hot," said Andy, moving across to Rupert's desk, which carried, among a host of other things, a tray with coffee cups. "Drink it up, Paula. We'll soon be having a meal. No, I don't think it was the main reason," he said again. "I think that your not-wanting-to-know mechanism had temporarily taken over and dimmed your light of reason. Because if you had guessed at blackmail you would also have guessed at the person most worth blackmailing. The one with the most to gain from Lady Hindon's death. You think it was Ernest whom Terry saw, don't you, Paula?"

"Yes. I assumed Rupert thought the same. We didn't mention names on the phone."

"You're right. Rupert believes that too. He's upstairs now, on the extension phone in his bedroom, talking to Ernest. His idea is to get Ernest to come and see him—or for him to go and see Ernest—and get him to confess. He thinks he might succeed, but he didn't think it wise to go alone. Hence the phone call to you, as the outsider, the person without an axe to grind."

"What about you? Did Rupert phone you too?"

"Not me. My mama. But she wasn't in. I answered the call, and I was so intrigued by Rupert's manner—very secretive, quite unlike himself—that I decided to drive over here as soon as I could and investigate. We've been doing a bit of talking, the two of us, but so far neither of us has convinced the other. That's where you come in."

"To give the casting vote?" Paula lit a cigarette. "Thanks for the coffee. I'm beginning to feel rather better. Why do you believe it wasn't Ernest?"

"I don't believe. I'm just uncertain. Listen, Paula. Terry was found about eight o'clock this morning by Bert, the head gardener. The doctor thought he'd been dead for at least twelve hours, more likely fifteen. That is, from about five o'clock yesterday afternoon. Both of them usually finish work at Merle House at four, but his mother says Terry has been coming home much later recently. Apparently he'd been lopping dangerous branches off the top of the apple tree, which Bert said was a job he was supposed to have done last week, and it looks as if he'd stepped off the ladder onto one of the rotten branches. There's no reason to suppose anybody else was involved, but the police have been asking a lot of questions. They feel there have been too many fatal accidents concerning people connected with Merle House."

Paula nodded. Her own belief had begun to waver a little as Andrew was talking, but it was best to hear him out to the end before speaking.

"Of course everybody concerned swears they were nowhere near Merle House at the time, that Terry must have fallen," he went on. "Me, Rupert, Melanie, Bruce, Ernest, my mama—you name them, they were somewhere else and can prove it. Including Dr. Glenning, of course, who was in London."

"Five o'clock yesterday afternoon," said Paula. "I'd got home and was reading my mail, but I can't prove it."

"Didn't you speak to anybody?"

"No. Oh, sorry. Yes, I did. I'd forgotten. I spoke to the girl in the downstairs flat. I'd let in her cat at the front door."

"Then presumably she will vouch for you. Not that anybody is seriously suspecting you of pushing Terry out of an apple tree, but it's as well to be prepared."

Paula made no reply. She was longing for Rupert to come down, but at the same time she was very anxious to hear all that Andy had to say.

"Ernest says he was with my mama. At his house."

"And your mother?"

Paula looked up at him as she asked this. Did he hesitate? Did he look doubtful? It was difficult to tell, with Andy.

"My mother says she was at Ernest's house with him. From about half past four right on through the night, and that he never left the house. She may well be speaking the truth."

Paula, who had been holding her breath, let it out in a sigh. "Oh, I do hope so, with all my heart," she said.

"Yes. Well, that's how it is."

Andy looked embarrassed again and began to fidget about the room, rearranging the collection of china dogs that Melanie had toyed with in her nervousness two days ago.

"Then if not Ernest," said Paula, "who do you think?"

Andy did not look at her as he replied. "Jill and Bruce both swear that they were at Jill's place all evening and all night. There is no independent witness to vouch for either of these two couples."

He replaced the china animal that he was holding—it was a Dalmatian, Paula noticed, about four inches long—and sat down opposite her.

"Bruce," muttered Paula. "If only it were Bruce whom Terry saw."

There was a silence. Paula shut her eyes. Weariness had overtaken her again. She ought not to have come. She was not going to be any use to anybody. That was the worst of being still convalescent. You felt perfectly all right and fit for anything, and then suddenly you weren't.

"Rupert's being an awfully long time," she said, opening her eyes and shifting slightly so that she could see Andy. "Are you sure he's still there? Could he have gone out without us hearing?"

"That's exactly what I'm wondering myself." Andy got up. "I'm going up to see. It's half an hour at least since he went to phone. Just before you arrived."

He left the room, rather to Paula's relief. She poured more coffee—it was only lukewarm now, but better than nothing—and ate a couple of biscuits, and began to feel a little more relaxed. It was good to have Andy here. Of all the people she had met in the neighbourhood it was he whom she most trusted. He was, like herself, an outsider, interested for his mother's sake, but extremely unlikely to be the subject of either Lady Hindon's generosity or her malice, and therefore extremely unlikely to have had any motive for killing her.

In fact, she trusted him more than she did Rupert. After all, Rupert had been connected with Merle House for a long time. He was right in the middle of that particular "set." She had been greatly relieved, even a little flattered, by his phone call asking for help. She had not questioned his sincerity. But supposing—just supposing—

Andy returned to the room. "He's not there," he said abruptly. "He's not in the house. He must have gone down the other staircase—this is two old cottages knocked together, you know—and gone out the side door."

Paula stood up. "Andy—you don't think it possible that Rupert—?"

There was no need to finish the question.

"I do think it possible," he said. "I've been trying to hint this to you ever since you arrived."

"But he's so very—"

"The original Mr. Nice Guy. It wouldn't be for personal gain. It would be to rid the world of a menace. Or a mercy killing."

"Terry wouldn't be a mercy killing."

"No. That's the big argument against this theory."

"And where has he gone now?"

"I don't know, Paula. I don't know what to do at all. What do you suggest?"

"I should absolutely love.to have something to eat and then go to bed, but of course that's out of the question. Perhaps we'd better phone Ernest and find out whether Rupert really did speak to him."

"Good suggestion. I've got his number somewhere." Andy sat down and reached for the telephone on the coffee table. "Mama seems to be spending most of her time there, so I keep it handy."

The line was busy. He had to try several times before he got through. The conversation was not very long. Paula could guess very little of its content from hearing only Andy's side of it.

"Ernest says Rupert did phone him," he said slowly, as he replaced the receiver. "But it was not for the reason we thought. I don't think Rupert has been honest with us. I'm inclined to believe Ernest."

"But what did he *say*?"

Paula's weariness had temporarily vanished. She was on her feet again and looked as if she was going to shake Andy if he didn't hurry up and tell her.

"Ernest says that Rupert just wanted to ask him one thing."

"And what was it? Don't be so *slow*, Andy."

"It was to ask if Ernest had seen Miss King's car anywhere near Merle House when he called there in answer to Lady Hindon's summons that afternoon."

"Miss King's car?" echoed Paula stupidly. And then she quickly recovered herself. "Melanie! Good heavens. That would explain a lot. Had Ernest seen it?"

"He noticed a little Fiat parked round the side, near the shrubbery. He thought it must belong to one of the temporary staff. He didn't recognise it as Miss King's, but he believes that hers is the same model."

"Andy, Andy." Paula was shaking him hard now. "This is it. Rupert's found out—it must have been after he talked to me—probably he only found out just now—that Melanie was there too that afternoon. I'm sure he's only just discovered it. Maybe she phoned him. Or he called her just before he called Ernest. And she said something—maybe she even confessed. Andy, this is it. Rupert's not trying to cover himself. He didn't kill Terry because he was blackmailing him. He wouldn't, he couldn't, kill Terry or anybody else. I'm sure he believed it was Ernest. But something Melanie said made him change his mind and that's why he's gone off without telling us. He's gone to see Melanie."

"You're only guessing," protested Andy when he could get a word in.

"I'm sure I'm right. Why should he disappear if he still believed Ernest guilty? Or Bruce? Or anybody else, except Melanie. Of course he wouldn't disappear. He'd have come straight down here to see me and we'd have had our talk. As we arranged on the phone. But Melanie—he's very protective towards Melanie. And she depends on him. If she were in trouble he'd go at once. And if he believed her guilty he wouldn't want anybody else to know. It makes sense, Andy."

He had to admit, after a little more excited persuasion from Paula, that it did.

"But would Melanie kill Terry?" he asked. "That sounds to me more like Bruce than any of the others."

This did bring Paula to a temporary halt, but she soon recovered.

"Melanie King is a very odd woman," she said. "And she's in a highly nervous state. Almost hysterical, I'd say. We've all been thinking it was because she gave Lady Hindon the medicine that helped to kill her."

"Maybe it did kill her. Maybe none of our suspects actually went in and finished her off with a cushion."

"Then what about Terry's fall?"

"Maybe it really was an accident."

"It wasn't. Terry was up to something. And with Melanie so often at Merle House he'd naturally think she'd be inheriting money. Perhaps she thought so too. Andy, I think we ought to go to Merle House. Now."

"Why not to Melanie's? She lives just up the road."

"All right. We'll go there on the way. But I'm sure we'll find no one there."

Paula was right. The little cottage, smaller even than Frances's, stood by itself half a mile from the village of Merle. It was in darkness and nobody answered the bell.

"I suppose we could break in," said Andy, surveying the porch with its festoons of climbing roses. "There seems to be a window open up there."

"No. Let's go to Merle House," said Paula.

"Okay. But if there's nothing happening there, then I think we ought to come back. We may find she's swallowed some of her own poisons."

"If she has, it'll be no kindness to try to revive her. Do hurry up, Andy."

"Mama is quite right," he grumbled as they got back into the old blue Vauxhall. "She said you were rather a bossyboots in spite of your small stature and your blue eyes and your air of sweet reason."

"I'm not bossy!" cried Paula very indignantly.

Andy laughed. "No, honey. I made that up to annoy you. Actually I'm very annoyed with myself because I think you're right about Melanie and I ought to have guessed and I didn't."

Whether because of his annoyance, or whether it was because he was getting very anxious himself, Andy covered the distance to Merle House at a most alarming speed, swung round into the drive with a painful screeching of brakes, and raced up to the front entrance.

There were two cars standing on the gravel. One of them was Rupert's mini; the other a little red Fiat. Lights shone from the house, and the library wing was uncurtained and all lit up. Paula was about to run up to the front door and ring the bell, but Andy restrained her.

"We can see into the library," he whispered. "We can probably hear too if we creep up close to a window."

"Good idea," murmured Paula, and followed him across the courtyard.

Beyond the area that was lit up by the lights from the house, the night was dark. They walked well away from the building until they were opposite the long window, and then they crept slowly forward, keeping in the shadow.

It was like looking at a brightly lit stage. There were only two characters in the scene, but they were certainly creating a lot of drama. One of them stood near the desk: a tall fair elderly woman who appeared to be in a state of extreme agitation.

She was talking—shouting, rather—at the other, and rummaging in the drawers of the desk as she did so.

"They're not here! But they must be here. She promised me—she promised me years ago that I should have her jewels when she died. She promised me!"

The voice was shrill and sounded alarmingly close. The listeners at the window tensed themselves.

Another voice, a man's voice, quieter but still perfectly audible, intervened.

"Melanie, you must come away now. You've no right to be here. Come. Let's go home, and you shall tell me all about it."

The man came into the watchers' line of vision while he was speaking. He was a stocky grey-haired man of medium height. He stretched out an arm towards the distraught woman and she roughly pushed him away.

"Leave me alone! It's my right. She promised me. I must have those jewels. She promised me!"

And she flung herself upon the desk, scattering papers, inkwell, blotter, and most of the rest of its contents onto the floor, and then proceeded to stamp on them, kick them, kick at the desk, pick up some of the remaining papers and tear them through, resisting all attempts of the man to calm her.

She seemed to have the strength of madness. Paula had a vision of her running riot through the library, tearing the books from the shelves, smashing the globe, pouring ink over the carpet.

"We've got to help Rupert," she whispered to Andy.

But it was too late. They had been so absorbed in the drama in the library, their ears so filled with Melanie's screaming, that they had not heard the car drive up nor the footsteps coming towards them.

"Stop there or I'll shoot!" shouted the newcomer.

It didn't seem to Paula that he was at ease in this particular role. In fact he sounded nervous, but a nervous man with a gun could be even more dangerous than a cool and calm one. So she stopped exactly where she was, rather uncomfortably, with one leg poised to step forward, feeling exceedingly nervous, in fact thoroughly scared, and afraid that this nervousness might cause her, most inappropriately, to laugh.

# —— 20 ——

Bruce came forward. He recognised them and put the pistol back into his jacket pocket.

"What the hell are you doing here?" he demanded angrily.

Paula had the feeling that he was as relieved as they were. But of course. He had taken them to be burglars—a whole gang of them—stripping Merle House in the absence of its guardian. No wonder he was nervous. It was brave of him to have challenged them at all.

"We thought we might help Rupert with Melanie," she explained. "Look."

Bruce looked through the window. Melanie was in the act of removing a very valuable vase from the mantelpiece and flinging it on the floor.

"Christ!" yelled Bruce, and attacked the window. "Let me in! Hurry up, you fool!"

Rupert rushed to let him in. Together they got to Melanie in time to stop two Staffordshire figures going the same way as the Chinese vase.

"Get the doctor," Bruce snapped at Paula. "Four-two-eight-six-zero."

Paula ran to the telephone, but stopped dialling when Rupert spoke. "There's no need. I'll take her home. See, she's quieter now."

Indeed, all the fight seemed suddenly to have gone out of

Melanie. She looked utterly bewildered, as if coming out of a dream. Bruce let her go, and Rupert kept an arm round her.

"I can manage now. I'll take her home. I'll call you later and explain. Sorry, Bruce. This was what I was trying to prevent. But the damage could have been much worse. I'll phone you as soon as I can. See you later, Paula. See you, Andy."

He led Melanie towards the window. "We'll go out this way. It's quicker."

"How did you get in?" Bruce called after them.

"Melanie has a key to the back door. She's had it for years. Lady Hindon gave it her."

"Good God." Bruce sounded stupefied. "I never knew. And I was supposed to be looking after the place."

"We'll help you clear up," said Andy. "Or do you need to leave it for insurance or something?"

Bruce appeared to take a grip on himself. "Don't let's bother with it now. Just check that that window is bolted. Thanks. Crazy—a place like this without any security system. But that's how she wanted it. The old man had guard dogs and plenty of staff on the premises. But her ladyship—oh, no. 'Bruce will look after me—I'm not afraid.' Silly old cow. I was afraid, even if she wasn't. God, am I glad it's all over."

Andy and Paula made sympathetic noises.

"Is Jill with you?" asked Paula.

"No. She's not up to it. Mrs. Flanagan's with her. I was going back there tonight, but in view of this—"

Bruce looked around at the devastation. It could have been much worse, but it was quite bad enough.

"I suppose I ought to call the police," he said. "But when it's a friend of the family . . . Oh, hell. Let's go and have a drink. It's comfortable in my flat. Not like this mausoleum."

How different he looks, thought Paula as they followed Bruce along the corridor, when you see him as his ordinary everyday self, and not as Lady Hindon's henchman or as a suspected murderer. This was how Jill saw him, no doubt. Competent and reliable, but full of nervous tension. A man who had been carrying a responsibility that he had not wanted; who had found it too much strain; who needed a tough woman like Jill to look after him.

Bruce led them down another corridor. His apartment was

on the ground floor at the back of the house, near to the door to which Melanie had a key.

"I'm going to bolt it after you've gone," he said. "For all I know, somebody else has keys. I always go in and out this way myself—it's nearer to the garage than the front door—and so do the staff, but I never knew that any of her friends came in that way."

"Did Lady Hindon have much jewellery?" asked Paula as they came into a big comfortable living-room with plenty of armchairs and tables, a few books, a huge television set, and a desk on which stood a computer with surrounding hardware.

Andy walked straight over to it.

"A Mackenzie?"

"Yes. A new model. I've just bought it."

There was satisfaction in Bruce's voice, and he looked as if he was going to expand on its merits to Andy, but fortunately he remembered that he had duties as a host. Whisky was produced and, to Paula's relief, some large slices of fruit cake. Now that the excitements of the last half hour were dying down, she was beginning to feel very hungry again.

"Bathroom's along the corridor," said Bruce before she had even asked him. "First on the left."

Paula told herself again that Bruce Wiley improved greatly on acquaintance.

"You were asking about the jewels," he said when she returned to the living-room. "They are mostly at the bank. She wore very little jewellery, and kept only a few pieces in the house. I never knew she'd promised anything to Melanie. She never mentioned it to me, and it's not in her will. Neither is Melanie. Neither am I." He took a long drink from his glass. "I could say something about that but I won't. Fortunately I have other resources and all I want now is to get the hell out of here and never see the bloody place again."

Paula and Andy said they could understand how he felt. Bruce had been carrying out one of those most thankless of tasks, involving responsibility without power, and his view of Merle House was bound to be very different from Frances's.

"How long will it be before you can go?" asked Andy.

"I promised the executors I'd stay on until after the inquest. If all goes well then, I'll hang on till the funeral. With luck it shouldn't be more than another fortnight, but if people are going to start coming and breaking the place up . . ." Again he drank. "Why didn't Melanie ask me about the jewels? I could have told her. I couldn't have helped her to them, but at least she needn't have done her housebreaking act."

"I suspect it's more complicated than that," said Paula. "I could make a guess at what's behind it, but I think it would be better to wait for Rupert. He knows all about it. He'll be able to explain everything."

"Then I wish he'd hurry up and do so. It looks to me as if Melanie's gone right off her rocker. She's always been somewhat cranky, but we thought it was harmless."

"You and Jill, you mean?"

"That's right." Bruce glanced at Paula. "I ought to have thanked you before, by the way, for rescuing her from hospital. She was practically climbing up the wall from frustration."

"And I ought to have apologised," said Paula, "for running off and leaving her the other afternoon. It was very rude of me and I've no excuse except that I hadn't fully recovered from the car crash and I seem to have been behaving rather oddly. I hope she's forgiven me."

"Oh, sure. Jilly doesn't hold grudges. Why doesn't that man call us?"

But they still had a little while to wait for Rupert's phone call, and when it came, it was simply to say that he didn't want to say anything on the phone, but would drive back to Merle House and be with them in fifteen minutes.

Bruce offered more drinks. Andy and Paula both refused, but wondered audibly whether there was any more cake.

"Haven't you had dinner?" asked Bruce.

They shook their heads.

"Hang on a minute."

He left the room and returned shortly afterwards with large hunks of bread and cheese, thus rising higher in Paula's estimation. Rupert arrived while she and Andy were stuffing themselves. He accepted the whisky, took a slice of bread and cheese, and sat down looking exhausted and extremely distressed. Bruce offered another drink and Rupert refused, adding, "I wonder—if it isn't too much trouble—I think I would like a cup of tea."

It was produced immediately.

When Rupert had somewhat recovered, he said, "I have just been acting in a way that is certainly illegal. Whether it is also immoral, you will have to judge for yourselves."

His listeners expected him to continue, but it was a full minute before he spoke again.

"Melanie King is a woman who has had very little of warmth or joy in her life. She and her sister were orphans, and I doubt whether anybody has ever loved her much, not even that sister whom she looked after with such devotion. After that death there remained two great passions in Melanie's life. One of them was for jewellery. The other was for Lady Hindon. Yes, truly. You'll remember we talked of it, Paula. I said that Melanie was probably the nearest that Lady Hindon had to a friend. Don't you agree, Bruce?"

"Me? Oh, sure. She was always hanging about the place. I assumed she was angling for a legacy, but I suppose she really did care for the old cow."

"You are right on both counts. She loved Lady Hindon and she looked forward to inheriting her jewels. She was promised them again and again, but by an oversight of Lady Hindon's—"

Bruce interrupted. "It wouldn't be an oversight. It would be sheer bloody-mindedness."

"That's possible, but it's also possible that she genuinely meant to include the bequest in her will, but whenever she saw the solicitor she was very preoccupied with her own feelings about the chief beneficiary. Ernest Brooker. Melanie just got forgotten. In fact that has been the story of her life except when somebody wanted something from her.

"Which is what happened when Lady Hindon decided she had had enough of it all. You knew she had such moods, Bruce?"

Bruce nodded. "We've had our dramas. Plenty of them. Even before tonight."

"But you didn't know that she had asked Melanie for something that would kill her, but that would not look as if she had either killed herself or taken too much of a drug by mistake?"

"No. I didn't know that."

"She had enormous vanity," said Rupert. "She couldn't bear to be thought weak or incompetent. She wanted it to look accidental, but she wanted to be sure. She also wanted something that would cause a lot of speculation, and that would annoy Dr. Mackeson. Melanie came up with the idea of a mixture of drugs. Lady Hindon doesn't seem to have been the least bit concerned about Melanie's position after the death, but apparently Melanie had enough sense of self-preservation to fix on a method that would not automatically get her accused of aiding and abetting a suicide.

"What she didn't know, because nothing in her nursing experience could tell her for sure, was how long the mixture would take to work. She was very worried about this. She was afraid Lady Hindon would be discovered too soon and resuscitated.

"That would mean great suffering and distress for Lady Hindon, and it would also mean that Melanie would never have the jewels, having failed so badly in her task. The two motives are so closely entwined that it is impossible to disentangle them, but I believe them to have been of equal strength —the poor woman's twin passions.

"That's why she came to Merle House that afternoon—to make sure that the job was done."

"But Rupert, just a minute," broke in Paula. "Lady Hindon had sent for Ernest. He thought she was going to tell him that she had disinherited him."

"Yes. She told Melanie that she was going to send for him and that the windows were to be left unlocked. But it was not to disinherit him. It was to say goodbye. She explained this to Melanie. He was the great love of her life, you see."

There was a short silence, broken by Andy. "Wasn't she afraid that Ernest would send for the doctor and have her revived?"

"He wouldn't have been told she was dying," replied Rupert. "She would have welcomed him, told him she was very tired, could only speak to him for a moment, but just wanted to see him. That's all she wanted. That Ernest himself might come under suspicion presumably never entered her mind.

"But in the event the farewell was never spoken. Melanie's mixture took effect sooner than was expected, and Ernest, in a fit of rebellion, arrived later than expected. He opened the library door, saw her, as he thought, fast asleep, and was only too glad of the excuse to go away.

"In fact she was already dead. Melanie had seen to that. She had come to check up on her before Ernest arrived. Lady Hindon was not breathing and there was no pulse, but Melanie felt it advisable to make completely sure. She took a cushion from the nearest armchair and held it firmly over the face for a while. Then she threw it back on the chair, checked again, decided that there was nothing more she need do, wept a little, kissed Lady Hindon, said, 'Goodbye, dear, I've done my best,' and left the library by the window, firmly believing that in the course of the next few days she would hear from the solicitors about the jewels."

There was another silence, again broken by Andy.

"But Terry Carson saw her?"

"Terry saw her. Instead of a nice letter from Bernard Smith's office she had a very nasty phone call from Terry. She agreed to meet him in the vegetable garden at Merle House between four-thirty and five o'clock yesterday afternoon. She arrived on the late side, and I suspect that Terry had become bored with waiting. At any rate, he seems to have decided that he might as well get on with one of his jobs—nobody has ever suggested that he wasn't a hard worker—so he got a ladder and set to work on the apple tree.

"When he saw Melanie approaching, he actually threw an apple at her, from up there on his perch, and it was this piece of cheekiness that cost him his life.

"She didn't mean to kill him, that I believe. But there is great violence in her, as you have seen for yourselves. This act of Terry's infuriated her and she rushed at the tree, pulled the ladder away, and then began to bang the ladder against the branches, shaking the whole tree and completely dislodging the loose branch on which Terry was balanced. It crashed down, bringing Terry with it.

"Melanie lost her head. She seems to have spent the next twenty-four hours in a state of shock and amnesia, shut up in her cottage, not answering the phone or the doorbell. Then, just before you arrived, Paula, she telephoned me. I was just about to call Ernest—at that time I was almost convinced that Ernest had a hand in Lady Hindon's death—and Melanie's call came when I was about to pick up the receiver. She was distraught. I did not know then what I now know, but it was obvious that her poor mind had given way completely. She wanted me to know that she 'had sinned,' and that she was going to Merle House 'to confess,' and that if she confessed, she would find the treasure.

"I questioned her, but she could not talk rationally. She'd said enough to make me very suspicious, though, and after making a brief call to Ernest I decided to go straight to Merle. I'm sorry, Bruce, that I didn't stop her from getting into the house and doing some damage, and I'm sorry, Paula and Andy, that I left you in the lurch and didn't tell you where I was going. But it was very urgent, and I couldn't have explained to you because I didn't understand it then myself."

"This seems to be the hour for apologising," said Bruce, turning to Paula. "I'll add one myself on behalf of Jilly. If she's given you any offence in any way, it was all done to protect me. She thought for a while that I'd finished off the boss myself."

"Well, now that we know," said Andy rather impatiently, "we can all stop suspecting each other. Poor Melanie. Where is she now, Rupert?"

"I don't know," he replied, slowly shaking his head. "In all truth I have to tell you that I don't know."

His three listeners stared at him. Paula was the first to grasp his meaning.

"She's dead. Is she dead, Rupert?"

"I would think it extremely likely."

"You mean you gave her the chance to kill herself?"

Rupert simply bowed his head.

"I see." Paula exchanged glances with Bruce and Andy. They all three looked, and felt, a little awed.

"Is that what you meant," went on Paula, "about possibly acting immorally?"

"Yes. I don't feel happy about it, but really I could not bring myself to do anything else."

"I don't call it immoral," said Paula. "I call it quite the opposite."

"Me too," said Andy. "I couldn't have done it myself—left somebody alone knowing they were going to suicide—but I'm very glad you did it. Aren't you, Bruce?"

Bruce was staring at Rupert. "You're a Minister of Religion, aren't you?"

Rupert made a grimace. "Yes."

Bruce held out a hand. "Then well done. Well done. It's good to know that one of them, at least, has more humanity than dogma."

"Thank you," said Rupert, producing a handkerchief and blowing his nose loudly. "Thank you all. Very much indeed."

A moment later he added, "Of course, I've got her signed confession. It was a relief to her to make it. I'll take it to the police tomorrow."

"It's tomorrow now," said Bruce, glancing at his watch.

Paula whispered something to Andy. He turned to Rupert. "I'm taking Paula back to Winsford with me," he said. "She'd love to come and stay with you another time, but not now. Besides, I've got a job for her. Ernest is threatening to refuse his legacy, and the dream of my mother's life is falling in ruins about her. Come on, Paula. This is where you came in. To be a comfort and support to my mama."

## About the Author

Anna Clarke was born in Cape Town, and educated in Montreal and Oxford. She holds degrees in both Economics and English Literature, and has held a wide variety of jobs, mostly in publishing and university administration. She is the author of twenty-one previously published suspense novels, including *Last Seen in London* and *Soon She Must Die*.